PUFFIN BOOKS

Editor: Kaye Webb

HIJACKED!

'This aircraft has been taken over by armed men
...'

Jason, flying back to school in England from
Hong Kong, was terrified when the plane was
hijacked. But when he found a way of escaping from
the plane (a way only he could take, because he was
an excellent swimmer), he realized that he must do
all he could to try to save his fellow travellers from
the revolutionary terrorists who held them hostage.

But getting outside was only part of it. In the
blistering heat of the South East Thailand coast
other attempts were being made to free the prisoners,
and Jason found he was the central figure in an
even more nerve-racking drama.

This most original adventure story (first published as *Jason*), with a highly topical theme,
will prove irresistible for readers of eleven and
over.

J. M. MARKS

HIJACKED!

Illustrated by Fermin Rocker

Puffin Books
in association with Oxford University Press

Puffin Books, Penguin Books Ltd, Harmondsworth, Middlesex, England
Penguin Books, 625 Madison Avenue, New York, New York 10022, U.S.A.
Penguin Books Australia Ltd, Ringwood, Victoria, Australia
Penguin Books Canada Ltd, 2801 John Street, Markham, Ontario, Canada L3R 1B4
Penguin Books (N.Z.) Ltd, 182–190 Wairau Road, Auckland 10, New Zealand

—

First published as *Jason* by Oxford University Press, 1973
Published as *Hijacked!* in Puffin Books 1977

—

Copyright © J. M. Marks, 1973
All rights reserved

—

Made and printed in Great Britain by
Cox & Wyman Ltd, London, Reading and Fakenham
Set in Intertype Baskerville

CONTENTS

I

A CHANGE IN COURSE

'TEN forty-six this time.' The man on the shore put the stop-watch back in his overcoat pocket. 'You're slowing down.' He looked at the boy resting on hands and knees in the shallows, wet skin steaming in the cold air. 'You've been at it long enough, Jason. Come on, we'll get home and wash off that salt water. Here.'

Still panting, the boy pushed himself up, splashed through the shallows and up on to the dry sand, took the huge white towel and began rubbing his face and chest.

'One thing about this training in the winter,' said his father, looking out over the empty beach and the grey waters of the bay, 'you've the whole place to yourself – nothing else but a few fishing junks.' He cocked an eye upwards at the heavy sound of a jet, invisible beyond the mass of apartment buildings and garden trees fringing the ridge behind. 'You'll be on one of those tomorrow. How d'you feel about going back to school?'

'All right.' Jason finished drying his legs, balanced on one foot while he dried sand from the other, slipped on rubber toe-sandals and began to dress. 'Pity the Christmas holidays are so short, though.'

'This Easter term's going to be a busy one for you,' his father went on. 'Your first "O" levels coming up – *and* this Southern Championship!'

'It's not the Championship itself, Dad.' Jason finished dressing, wrung out his swimming trunks and rolled them in the towel. 'That's in May. This is just to get selected for special training.'

'I can remember when you thought your junior school form races were the summit of everything!'

Jason smiled to himself. His father didn't really understand – but at least he was letting him go back a few days early in time for the all-important elimination heats this coming Saturday – a week today.

'Come along,' said his father. 'Keep moving, or you'll stiffen up and catch cold.' The two of them jogged up on to the road, climbed into the Morris and drove uphill past the Repulse Bay Hotel towards Mount Nicholson and their stone bungalow looking back south over the China Sea.

'There's one thing about Hong Kong,' remarked his father, switching on the headlights as they turned into the short drive, 'it may get cold but it's never quite freezing – just right, really, and a nice change from summer. Makes the year bearable.'

The lights in the bungalow were just being switched on and Jason saw the welcoming glow of a fire. He smiled again as he gave his damp hair a final quick rub. It was cold now that he'd stopped – and that long, hard swim had made him hungry.

'Tea and toast,' called his mother. 'You two'll be starving! You know,' she said to Jason, as she passed him the strawberry jam, 'two training sessions a day are too much. I don't know what the school will make of you when you get back. You've never taken swimming so seriously before! Why don't you just stick to swimming in the school baths?'

'I'm all right, Mum,' he said defensively, 'really I am – and training at sea, where there's a bit of choppy water, is twice the use of going up and down the baths, especially for the fifteen hundred metres!'

'Well, I don't know.' She spoke with resignation. 'I think you swim too much, and it's a shame to cut your holidays short. You'll be going back days before the others!' She sighed. 'However, at least your appetite's none the worse.'

'He eats like a sea-horse!'

Butter-knife in hand Jason paused and shot a scornful look across the table at his younger brother rocking from side to side at his own joke. 'Haven't noticed you exactly dying of starvation!'

'That's enough, you two.' Edgar Wright looked at his sons thoughtfully. They got on pretty well together, considering the four years that separated them, but it wasn't their occasional arguments that was occupying his mind – it was this new fetish of Jason's, this craze for swimming. The boy was certainly a remarkable swimmer for his age – something to do with his long legs and deep chest – but he was taking it so seriously – passionately, almost! Last summer he'd been full of the Olympics, and now he even seemed to have ambitions in that direction – what young swimmer wouldn't? But to talk, as the boy had done, of making a career of swimming – Edgar Wright frowned – that would be quite the wrong course for Jason. Daydreams were all very well, even at fourteen, but there were more important things to think about.

The next morning was raw and gusty with wind, with sudden bursts of rain splattering against the windows so fiercely that the casements rattled. 'We're not finished with the typhoons yet,' remarked Mr Wright as they sat down to their porridge. 'Looks as if we'll get the tail end of Typhoon Agnes after all. You'll miss it though,' he said to Jason, 'no typhoons where you're going.'

'But wasn't it heading out to sea?' Mrs Wright looked round as the wind drove rain in crooked paths across the glass. 'It's been on the move for days!'

'It came down the Formosa Strait past Taiwan and should have turned out to sea again, but didn't. Just as well the new tunnel's been completed – the harbour'll be choppy for the ferry this morning.' He finished up his cup of tea and rose from the table. 'We'll be off then. Got everything?'

The front door slammed behind him as he ran out to the garage, dragged open the door and hooked it back. The wind was gusting over the Peak and funnelling between the shoulders of the ridge where the Gap Road ran just above them, and eddies plucked at the door. He warmed up the car, backed it round, Jason swung his suitcase into the back, his mother and Andrew climbed in and, windscreen wipers working busily, they turned out of their drive and joined the stream of cars heading for downtown Hong Kong. Once through the new tunnel to the mainland and past the traffic of Kowloon they reached Kai Tak, its long peninsula of runway busy with jets of the world's airlines. Parking the car they hurried to the airport buildings, past construction sites where Hakka women laboured by hand next to modern machinery, the traditional black cloth fringes to their straw hats flapping wildly in the wind and rain.

The airport lounges were crowded with, it seemed, every nationality under the sun, and business at the long reception desks went on in a dozen languages, from Swahili to Cantonese, and there seemed to be a dozen groups of Chinese animatedly bidding farewell to young men and women bound for Europe.

Once checked in at reception Jason stood with his parents waiting for the call to the departure lounge. 'We'll be back for a month in the summer,' said his father. 'I'll let you know the dates well in advance. We might try a few days in Scotland this year.' They talked in desultory fashion till Jason's flight number was called. 'Well, goodbye, Mum – ' he kissed his mother, shook hands formally with his father and gave his brother's hair a friendly rumple. 'See you.'

'I'm always uneasy till he's reached Heathrow,' confessed his mother, as she watched Jason through the glass partition of the departure lounge.

'Don't be – these V C10s are very reliable. Don't look so concerned! This time tomorrow he'll be with his uncle in Hampshire, talking to him about swimming!'

For a moment or two Mrs Wright did not reply, but stood gazing absently at the line of passengers queuing to have their passports examined and their luggage inspected. There were Indian and Pakistani businessmen, two Koreans, several Chinese, a Malay wearing a smart black songkok in contrast to his European suit, a pair of English children in charge of the stewardesses, Europeans dressed in warm clothes and carrying overcoats in preparation for the January weather of Heathrow, and a group of Japanese – three men in neat grey suits and two women in traditional kimono and obi, their long black hair carefully arranged in smooth buns. It was this group that drew Mrs Wright's attention, and she pointed them out to her husband: 'They look so much nicer in traditional dress, don't they, Edgar? Those kimonos are really attractive.'

'Indeed they are.' He smiled. 'But those young women still haven't forgotten to put on modern powder and paint!'

'Nonsense – they've hardly any! And, besides, it helps when one's travelling – they're probably worried about flying, poor things. Look how solemn they are!'

'They're generally pretty solemn, these Japanese. Ah, there's Jason now, by the passport desk.' He waved and Jason, catching the movement, turned and waved back, then moved on to be checked.

As soon as their passports had been examined, they were ushered towards the electronic metal detector and their hand luggage searched. 'Everything metal to be shown, please – everything metal.' The call was repeated and waiting his turn Jason watched as the passengers produced watches, key rings, cigarette cases, coins, trinkets, nail-clippers, powder compacts, manicure sets, a baby transistor radio – the Europeans with resignation, the Indians and Pakistanis with indifference, the Chinese with a faint air of amusement, the Japanese gravely and conscientiously and the Koreans with grim, defensive looks. At last all were through and then came the call to the aircraft.

As they entered the Super VC10, parked against the high passenger pier, Jason saw that his seat was well aft – much handier for the washrooms. He also noted with relief that this flight would not be too crowded. There were hardly more than sixty passengers – an average midwinter load. He'd be able to stretch out a bit across the empty seats. He was also glad to be going back early for another reason: the returning school flight was always crammed and sometimes boisterous, which could be tiresome. It was really rather a relief to be going back with a bunch of adults, no matter how dull-looking. At least there was less likelihood of waking from an uneasy sleep with a dollop of ice-cream sliding down one's back.

In the seat next to the window in his row sat a middle-aged Chinese and across the central gangway were the two children he'd seen earlier. With the passengers settled the stewardesses – one of whom was Chinese – came round with shallow baskets of sweets and, that final routine over, the great door closed. 'Fasten seat belts' flashed on above him, the paired engines at the tail started up, and the aircraft moved out on to the flight path.

Although used to flying, Jason still felt a tremor of apprehension as the engines revved up and take-off began. He was pressed back in his seat as the aircraft climbed, his stomach seemed to fall away with the dwindling harbour below, but soon the sharp climb levelled out, the signal for seat belts was switched off and busy movement by the stewardesses began. He leant forward and took the glossy airline brochures from the pocket in front of him. 'Welcome Aboard Speedwing II' announced the first; 'Route Map and Flight Information' announced the second; but these he put back, opening with anticipation a smaller folded card which simply said 'Menu'. His morning porridge seemed long past. The card read: 'Hong Kong – Bangkok: Breakfast for Joining Passengers'. He glanced round; the stewardesses were moving up the gangway with their trolleys. He studied the menu carefully. As usual, the main difficulty was choice. There was fresh fruit appetizer, grilled Waikato ham steak, sauté of kidney with mushrooms, crusty roll, butter, croissants, jam and coffee or tea. Soon a stewardess had reached his seat and the businessman next to him, after a word or two in Chinese, settled for the ham steak and coffee. Then the girl turned smiling to Jason: 'Breakfast — what would you like?'

He resisted the impulse to say: 'The lot', and settled for the fruit appetizer, the ham steak, rolls and coffee.

Just in front three young Englishmen — junior staff of one or other of Hong Kong's business houses — interrupted their talk to begin a hearty breakfast, and across the gangway the two children were being tempted to eat by the stewardess. The girl, two or three years older than her brother and very much in charge of him, accepted a glass of pineapple juice, helped her brother with his, then gradually relaxed, accepting a croissant while he cheerfully tucked into everything the stewardess proffered. With breakfast over, the public address system buzzed briefly then a voice said: 'Good morning: this is the Captain speaking . . .' He welcomed them aboard, announced their height and speed, gave the weather conditions and the estimated time of arrival in Bangkok, and wished them a pleasant journey.

It was cooler, and Jason thought of his pullover. Other passengers were reading or chatting and some were already dozing off. Next to him the middle-aged Chinese reclined his seat and lay back and was soon breathing regularly. Through the window Jason saw below them only cloud, a brilliant white. He began to realize how early he'd been up. He too reclined his seat and leant back.

He woke an hour later, glanced at his watch and remembered he'd have to spend the rest of the journey continually putting the hands back as they crossed the lines of longitude. The man beside him was still asleep. Forward the first-class cabin curtain parted, and a tall man with a fair beard, wearing four gold rings on his blue uniform sleeve, walked down the gangway greeting the passengers. He paused at Jason. 'Back to school?'

' 'Fraid so.' Jason grimaced politely.

'You're early – the school rush isn't usually for another week!'

'I've some swimming heats on Saturday – Southern Championship trials.'

'Good luck! By the way, is this your first trip out?'

'No. My father's in the Agricultural Department. We've been all over the place – Borneo, Malaya and now Hong Kong.'

'You're well travelled, then!' The Captain moved on with a nod and a smile and Jason settled back, thinking of the coming heats. With all that training in the chilly waters of Repulse Bay he'd have a better than average chance. Then, if he got through, there would be training for the spring regional competitions, but his thoughts moved beyond even those, and in his ears boomed the Olympic roar. If he trained steadily and built up his strength he might well manage a time of under seventeen minutes by May and make the British long-distance team before he left school – possibly even sooner. His coach, normally a silent man, was enthusiastic. Jason leant back, dreaming of the crowds, the pale green water, the television lights and the joyous pain of effort.

'Coffee – or perhaps something soft to drink?' The stewardess glanced at the sleeping Chinese next to him and lowered her voice. He thanked her and took a coke. She did not move on, however, but leant to whisper confidentially: 'You're Jason, aren't you? I'm Sue. You're travelling alone – I wonder if you'd help us and spend a few minutes with those two children?' She nodded round to where the brother and sister sat leaning back in their seats, the little boy looking solemnly at the seat ahead while his sister sat more stiffly, determination fighting her apprehension. 'Their parents were injured in a car crash on the road over Tai Mo Shan three days ago. They're going home to relatives, and they're feeling very much alone.'

'Of course.' He met the little girl's wary look. Beside her the little boy was fidgeting uncomfortably. 'Oh, God,' thought Jason, 'he's going to be sick.' His heart sank a little.

'There's a seat beside them,' whispered the stewardess as she led him over, 'and here are some picture books. Will you read them something?'

'All right,' he agreed without enthusiasm. He felt that this wasn't exactly the job for him – more a girl's – but he'd promised.

'Wonderful.' Sue smiled her thanks and moved on, and with a sigh he settled into the seat and looked down to meet the inspection of the little girl. He put on rather a strained smile: 'What's your name?'

'Margaret.'

'And your brother's?'

'John. What's your name?'

'Jason.' He watched with a twinge of amusement as she sat looking sideways up at him, doubt struggling with disbelief. At length she said: 'Jason?'

'Yes. Not many boys are called Jason,' he explained, 'but it's my real name. Now,' he went on briskly, 'let's see what there is to read.'

He opened the first picture book, *A Tale of a Tiger,* and his heart sank further. He looked round furtively; suppose anyone saw him with this stuff! But he'd promised, and with another glance round he began: 'In the far jungles of Bengal – ' He stopped, clearing his throat while the little girl looked at him critically, still defensive. She couldn't have been more than six, he thought, and she was reading him as easily as he read the book. He took a dogged breath: 'In the far jungles of Bengal,' he said again, 'there lived a family of tigers . . .' The pages were mainly taken up with beautifully drawn pictures of two mild-looking tigers of great size, and a fluffy-pawed tiger-cub with round eyes that stared out at him in astonishment. This imbecile-looking cub, he learnt as he read, was the main character, Tig, and he seemed to spend his time getting into un-tiger-like scrapes.

'He's spotty,' observed the little girl. 'He should have stripes!' She returned his look with a haughty stare.

Jason turned the page and there it was – a picture telling how Tig grew stripes from his baby spots. 'You've heard this before,' he accused.

'No,' she said loftily. 'Tigers *should* have stripes.'

He took a deep breath and with a rueful grin read on – and as he read he found it wasn't a bad story at all; it had a beginning, some amusing twists and quite a good ending. He read with a growing, if guilty, interest, pausing while the little girl laughed in pleasure. Her young brother laughed as well, though dutifully rather than through comprehension. And he hadn't been sick, either!

'Here you are, Jason, and you, Margaret, and young John!'

Jason looked up in surprise – he too had been in Bengal with Tig and his adventures. The stewardess gave him her secret smile. 'I've brought you three something.' She handed them each a tall glass holding a frothy concoction of ice cream crowned with fruit, chopped nuts and a tracery of chocolate, and with straws and long silver spoons. 'We call this our Speedwing Special,' she confided. 'Only very special passengers get it.' She bent and whispered to Jason. 'Good work. I think they'll sleep a little now, but perhaps later – ?'

'Yes, I'll read them some more.' He waited till they had all downed their Speedwing Specials and then moved back to his own seat. He looked round. The little boy was leaning back, eyes closing, with his sister importantly wiping a fringe of chocolate from his mouth. She settled back, caught his eye, and smiled, no longer defensive. 'Good kids,' he thought, and smiled back.

The cloud base parted briefly as they passed near Hainan and then closed in once more. 'Bangkok soon.' Jason looked at his watch, and looked around. Above the seats he could see only the tops of heads – the black, carefully groomed hair and ivory foreheads of the Chinese and Thai businessmen, the fair hair of the Europeans, the cropped Koreans, and the smooth black hair of the Japanese ladies. He began to feel sleepy again, but blinked to stay awake. He'd hang on and sleep in darkness – it was always better to avoid sleeping in daylight on these long flights. He yawned and stretched, noticing without interest that two passengers – a Japanese and his wife – were following a stewardess through into the first-class compartment. They'd be having the first conducted tour of the flight deck, he guessed, yawning again, then smiled to himself as he saw the man pause fractionally at the doorway and duck his head in a bow. Always formal and polite, thought Jason; how do they keep it up? He forgot them as he peered past the sleeping Chinese, trying to see down through the cloud cover.

'Captain – Captain Chisholm.'

Forward on the flight deck the Captain looked up as the stewardess touched his shoulder. 'Yes, what is it?' He looked from her pale face to the man behind her, a man who bowed formally but whose hand held the razor edge of a scalpel to the stewardess's neck. Behind him the woman, also with a fractional bow, zipped open a blue plastic airline bag, and showed the Captain a slab of pale, putty-like material. Captain Chisholm's eyes fastened on the slab, the cork-shaped, cottony-white plug embedded in it, the glint of a detonator and short lengths of wiring connected to one end of a series of torch batteries. Below

18

the delicately plucked eyebrows the narrowed brown eyes were hard as stone.

The Captain drew a long breath of resignation and nodded. The man leant forward to the control column, and flicked the radio transmission switch above the Captain's left thumb back to 'Intercom'. With a warning gesture of the scalpel he indicated: 'Do not transmit', then handed him a sheet of paper inscribed in Japanese ideographs, with below them, typed in English capitals, 'FLY BEARING 180'. The Captain sighed and passed it to his co-pilot, who had been scrutinizing the bag of explosive dangling some inches from his left ear. He gave a slight shrug of acceptance and set the new course.

Back in the tourist cabin Jason felt the big aircraft bank and turn, looked out of the window and saw the cloud swing slowly round. 'Bangkok already?' They'd be stacking up, probably waiting for ground clearance. He settled back in his seat without much interest: Bangkok's Don Muang was like most airports – hot and boring; but it was a change from dozing away in an aircraft, no matter how comfortable. He glanced round at the children again, and saw the stewardess had strapped them into their safety harness and reclined their seats, and that both were sound asleep. Next to him the Chinese still slept, but in front one of the English passengers was looking out of a window and saying something to his neighbour, and they compared watches. He pressed the call-button and when no stewardess appeared pressed it again, looking round back down the long gangway. Then the door from the first-class compartment opened and Sue appeared. He held up an arm, 'Miss, we've changed course –'

She forced a smile: 'The Captain will be making an announcement,' and hurried aft.

By the galley the second stewardess and the bar steward sat very quietly in their seats, with beside them in the galley the second Japanese woman and the two remaining men. One was opening out a packet of explosive while the other, neatly and carefully, was making it up into smaller packages, each with a cork-shaped, cottony white primer, then shredding open the cigarettes in his case to reveal slim shiny detonators which he inserted into the primers. Finally he took a length of insulated wire from beneath the belt round his trousers, snipped it into 12-inch lengths and wired the detonators to paired torch batteries. He worked steadily, absorbed in his task, not lifting his head when over the intercom came the Captain's voice: 'I have an important announcement for all passengers.'

Heads turned up towards the loudspeakers. Jason looked at the sleeping man next to him, guessed that he might not understand much English and decided to leave him. But what was going on?

'Please pay careful attention.' The voice was matter-of-fact and impersonal. 'This aircraft has been taken over by armed men and I am now under their orders. I will follow these implicitly, and everything possible will be done to ensure the safety of all on board. Please remain in your seats as far as possible, with your safety belts fastened. I will keep you fully informed of all developments. Thank you.'

The shocked silence that followed was broken by a hubbub of talk and ripples of movement as heads poked up above the seats, looking round.

Hijacked! Jason found it hard to believe. He looked round cautiously, not putting his head up too far, expecting to see men standing at the end of the cabin holding machine-guns or revolvers or grenades, but to his surprise he saw nothing. Then he remembered: those two Japs who had followed Sue . . .

But where were they heading? What did the hijackers want? Then he realized with a shock: if this went on too long he'd miss his vital heats; he'd be set back a whole year, that vital year without which there might be no Olympics for him. He visualized the process: touchdown at Bangkok, the long wait on the hot tarmac apron; floodlights, bargaining, the hijackers' demands met at last and then the reporters, the interviews . . . He fidgeted. Everything depended on how long this all took.

Beside Jason the sleeping Chinese stirred and opened his eyes, grunted and rubbed his face. Then with a murmured apology he heaved himself from his seat, and Jason swung his legs into the aisle to let the man past, heading down for the washrooms aft, yawning as he went. A few moments later he returned, wide awake, looked at Jason doubtfully, opened his mouth once or twice as if uncertain whether to speak and at last said, 'Not going Bangkok.'

Jason looked at him in surprise. This chap hadn't understood, hadn't quite grasped what was going on. 'We are going to Bangkok,' he said patiently, 'but – ' he paused, wondering how to explain other than with slang, could think of nothing better and said, 'Hijacked.'

'Hijack I know.' The Chinese nodded. 'But not going Bangkok.' He gestured. 'Look at sun.'

At first Jason did not grasp his meaning then, looking out of the porthole, saw the sun high to their left, and understood. They were flying south.

2

BEACHED

SOUTH! Jason snatched out the route map and rapidly flicked over the pages till he reached Map E – South-East Asia. Southwards the map showed two big airports, Singapore and Kuala Lumpur, and Singapore, he decided, was where the hijackers were taking them; instinctively he felt that they would choose somewhere near the sea. He craned to look past the Chinese out through the window. Somewhere beneath that layer of brilliant white cloud was the Gulf of Siam. He looked at his watch. They must have turned south just short of Bangkok. According to the route map Singapore was 814 miles south of the Thai capital – that meant another hour and a half in the air before they reached Singapore – and when all this was over, they'd probably have to fly all the way north again. He thumped his knee in frustration. He might very well miss the heats altogether.

He stood up and looked aft. The stewardesses had moved forward to the last row of seats, and in their places by the after-door and galley were three of the hijackers – two men and a woman in a kimono. The other passengers sat quietly enough, apparently resigned, but in front of him the young Englishmen were deep in talk. Occasionally one or other of them glanced carefully back at the three Japanese, and Jason caught snatches of their muttered conversation: ' – no weapons that I can see.'

' – holding something on her lap – explosives?'

'Maybe they're bluffing.'

22

'Maybe.'

Then he saw that the children had woken and were looking about. Remembering his promise he slipped across to them. 'Like me to read to you again?'

Their faces, bemused by sleep, lit up, and he looked at them with a pang. They had as yet no idea that anything was wrong.

'Jason,' murmured the little boy, blinking.

'What would you like? We've had the tiger story – I'll look for something else, shall I?'

'No.' Margaret shook her head firmly. 'The tiger.'

'Very well, then.' Jason smiled. Once more wouldn't hurt. He fastened himself into the seat beside them, but though he spoke the words his attention wandered. What did the hijackers want? Clearly they weren't escaping from anywhere, for they must have had valid passports and fares. No, it would be the usual demand for some political release; some Japanese prisoner would shortly be let go and they'd all be free to travel on again – but he wished that the hijackers had simply settled for Bangkok. He looked at his watch: it was one o'clock Hong Kong time, another forty minutes or so to Singapore.

Forward on the flight deck Captain Chisholm was also checking his watch. He had just noticed that it was a second or two after one when the woman thrust a square of coloured chart down at him and he examined it, first with curiosity, then with close attention. It was a section cut from a large-scale Ordnance Survey sheet overprinted with air-photo reconnaissance detail, and one spot, its co-ordinates inked in beside it, had been arrowed. He looked in doubt up at the woman, then studied the map again. At length he handed her the map back, shaking his head and saying slowly and clearly: 'No good. Sorry – no can do.' He dropped his right hand to the auto-throttle but felt the prick of a scalpel point on his neck and looked up again.

The plastic bag of explosive was open, a hand held the contact wire and stony brown eyes stared into his own. For a long moment they stared at each other till, reluctantly, the Captain nodded acceptance.

Jason was talking to the children and was asking them whether they had yet learnt to swim when he grabbed at his arm-rests and they were pressed back in their seats as the aircraft made a long, ninety-degree banking turn to starboard. The aircraft levelled out and heads turned up as the public address system was switched on with a click and a rustle. 'Ladies and Gentlemen,' the Captain's voice was flat and unemotional. 'I have been ordered to make an emergency landing. This should be in about eight minutes, and it may be bumpy.' He cleared his throat, paused a moment, then went on: 'I want you all to pay careful attention to these instructions. Please undo all clothing that is tight or constricting. Remove shoes, slacken off ties and braces, open shirt collars, take off and put away spectacles. Got that? Finally, when we are about to land, I will call out to you to brace, and I want you to raise your knees up and wrap your arms around your heads. Now, slacken off that clothing.' He switched off, and at once there was a ripple of activity as ties were removed, collars opened and clothing slackened and the stewardesses hurried along the gangway, ensuring that everyone complied. Jason busied himself with the children: 'We'll get your sandals off,' he said, trying to make his voice encouraging, adding: 'When I tell you, you must curl up tight, in a little ball.'

The children had caught the tension; John huddled quietly in his seat, but his sister called out with a slight break in her voice: 'This is not where we're going!'

Jason tried to reassure her: 'We're just going to stop for a little while.' But he spoke with stiff lips and knew that she saw the fear in his face. He felt a tap on his shoulder:

24

'I'll take over now.' It was Sue. She moved the children apart and strapped herself in between them, while Jason moved back to his own seat. He gave a last glance round as he tightened his seat belt. The few faces he could see appeared bored or merely irritated and he wondered if underneath they too felt the cold, sick apprehension that gripped him from throat to stomach.

The loudspeaker clicked and rustled: 'Going down now!' and the aircraft's nose went down and they began to lose height. Down and down they went, the brilliant sunshine vanished – they flew through wet grey cloud – and then they were out into the sunshine again, with the sea close below them. But the sea broke against a beach, a long white beach with a forested ridge rising beyond its farther end and an open plain of lallang grass opening back from the nearer side, pale green against the dark trees. From above they saw the long outline of a runway along it, a grass runway beside a collapsed bamboo shack, and it was for this runway that they were heading.

'There's no proper airfield!' shouted one of the men in front.

'Hell!' Another grabbed the back of his seat as he turned to point down. 'That's only an emergency strip! We're – '

Jason did not hear the rest of his sentence. He was staring down to starboard as the aircraft banked again. The man was right: there was no proper landing field, only an overgrown grass strip no more than a thousand yards long. He felt his stomach contract. Their huge aircraft, designed for a broad concrete runway over a mile in length, was heading down straight for this brief ribbon of green with the white sand beside it, on one side the forest, on the other the sea.

He ignored the popping in his ears and stared down. They were much lower, and he saw the ridge, the long white beach and the landing strip – uneven and over-grown with tall lallang grass – and then the ridge again, thickly covered by the crowding tops of huge trees. As the aircraft banked and turned, he twisted his head, looking for any sign of a town or village, but there was only the forest, the sea and that short strip of green.

Down they went till they were skimming over trees; he glimpsed palm tops, then heard a shout of 'Brace! Brace! Brace!' clamped himself into a little ball and was jerked forward hard into his seat-belt as the Captain applied reverse thrust in the air with a violent braking effect. For a moment the aircraft seemed to pause and hang then, bump! it touched ground and sprang into the air; bump! it touched again and the undercarriage quivered, and then they were down and bumping fast along the strip. Jason buried his head more deeply in his folded arms; he was mentally counting off the hundreds of yards and visu-alizing the forest trees which stood at the far end; they must be nearly up on them, and the aircraft was still hurtling along. The engines howled in reverse thrust, it was no good, they wouldn't stop in time, Jason braced himself for the crash – and then he felt the aircraft swing and fractionally change direction. They burst through a screen of clumps of lallang grass and the huge machine rocked from side to side as it ploughed diagonally down the beach. Sand sprayed up past the windows and scoured the metal body, but now the sand was mixed with spray as the great paired wheels ploughed on through shallow water, till at last Speedwing II shuddered to a halt, gouts of steam hissing up from the hot jets and sea-water pour-ing down from wings and fuselage.

At once the hijackers aft threw off their seat belts and the two men hurried to open the door, while the woman holding the explosive stood on guard in the gangway. Someone shouted 'Now!' and the three passengers in front of Jason raced down the gangway and sprang at the Japanese. The biggest seized the woman's arms from behind and grappled with her, trying to twist the package away, and the two Japanese men were carried back against the row of seats by the rush. The nearest hijacker struck back at his assailant, who dodged the blow and punched him hard full in the face. Blood spurted and the man fell back again but with an immediate reflex action his foot snapped up and the toe of his smart black shoe caught the Englishman in the left ribs. With a gasp of pain he doubled up, the Japanese followed up with another kick, then rose and struck repeatedly and accurately at neck and head till he collapsed. The second Englishman fared little better. His first punch was parried, his wrist was seized, pulled sharply and then twisted up behind his back in one smooth movement. As he strained down, a short palm-jab broke his jaw and left him unconscious on the metal deck.

In the gangway the big man still held the woman round the neck from behind. Unable to wriggle free from his powerful grip she drove her elbow hard back into his ribs. He gasped, winded; she rocked forward then back, and as he lost his balance, she dropped her right shoulder, bent her right knee, and in one swift movement pulled forward and down, with the result that he was catapulted over her shoulder to land heavily with a clatter of crockery in the opposite section of the galley. She tried to step back but from the floor he grabbed her kimono, and, panting with rage, she kicked at him, but her padded sandals had little effect. He pulled himself to his feet, still grasping her kimono, and she staggered under his weight.

'Sashi!' came a shout as the big man seized her left arm and tried to wrest away the package, 'sashi korosé!'

'Hai!' From her sash she snatched out a scalpel, swung it up and plunged it into his chest.

'Aah!' His grip slackened and she turned and made for the gangway, but with a clumsy grab he seized her hair, twined his fingers into the bun and gave a desperate jerk. There was a sound like silk tearing, and he tumbled backwards with a long black wig in his right hand, with staring round at him the cropped head of a young Japanese man, his face suddenly grotesque in its disguise of rouge and powder.

The big man caught his breath painfully as he moved. Blood was seeping through his shirt and he put a hand to his chest. He sank down, breathing with difficulty, blinking up at the man with the scalpel, then turned his face against the smooth stainless steel of the galley cupboard and lay there with his eyes closed, while blood trickled from his chest. The Japanese pulled the wig from the big man's fingers, began to put it on, then with a sudden imprecation flung it down and, scalpel in hand, stamped his way out of the galley again.

It was all over in less than a minute.

His eyes peering just over the back of his seat, Jason watched the failure of the attack with despair. The sudden explosive violence of the Japanese hijackers appalled him; their strutting confidence as they trod over the two men groaning on the cabin floor and their unspoken challenge to anyone else to try made his heart sink. Just as if there had been no interruption the two hijackers returned to the door while the third man – grimly menacing in his disarranged kimono and painted face – kept watch. The door bolts were pulled, the handle jerked open and, at a brief word, one man leapt the ten feet down to the shallow water like a cat, then splashed his way under the fuselage. The other two returned to their seats where they sat staring stonily at any passenger who turned his head to look. A steward got up and began to edge his way towards the two injured men but a blade lifted and he sat down again.

From where he sat Jason could see a patch of sandy shore sloping gently up to a line of palms, with beyond them tall, pale green bushes edging the forest. The hijacker who had jumped down was still invisible, but Jason heard him call, and a second man jumped down to help him. Behind Jason a steward muttered: 'They're at the after luggage bay.' There was a scraping, the clang of a metal hatch door swinging open and a moment or two later a hijacker ran forward under the wing holding a sub-machine-gun and two green-painted grenades. He returned empty-handed, disappeared under the fuselage again, reappeared with another sub-machine-gun under his arm and signalled to the man with the painted face. He leapt down and was given this weapon and a grenade, and the others joined him in taping explosives under the fuel tanks.

'Quick – ' The bar-steward and Sue sprang to deal with the injured. At the same time the forward door opened and the half-dozen first-class passengers filed in, followed by Captain Chisholm and the flight crew.

'Captain – along here, Sir!' The bar-steward waved urgently, and the Captain ran to him and stared at the two men on the deck and then at the steward. 'They had a go, Sir,' he explained, 'and there's one worse, lying in the galley.'

'When did this happen?'

'Just as we switched off. One of them shouted, and then they charged down.' The steward told what he had seen of the fight, and Captain Chisholm pushed into the galley and knelt among the bloodstained crockery to undo the injured man's shirt. 'Puncture wound,' he said grimly, 'deep, and in a bad place.' He looked up into the steward's anxious face. 'We must get him out of this. If he lies there much longer, he'll bleed into his lungs and choke.'

'But where, Sir? There's not a lot of room in the cabin, now, with everyone pushed into just this one!'

'We'll have to get the injured down into the shade of that wing, where there's room and a bit of breeze. I'll let those Japs know.' He leant out of the open passenger door and waved down at the hijackers. Two were crouched at a big transistor radio, its aerial fully extended, but the third man, with a word to the others, raised his sub-machine-gun. The Captain gestured back to the galley, indicating that the injured should be laid out under the wing. The Japanese made no move and the steward said: 'I'll get down there, sir; we'll have to lower 'em slowly.' He sat on the deck, ready to push himself out, and the muzzle of the sub-machine-gun swung towards him. He paused. 'They don't understand, Sir.'

'They understand, all right. Come back from there.'

'I'll just try once more.' The steward made as if to jump down, and the Japanese lowered his muzzle slightly and fired a short burst. The bullets passed close beneath the fuselage, and at the high-pitched shattering noise women in the cabin screamed. The steward scrambled away from the door. 'Here,' he said shakily, 'they're not human!'

'I told you,' said Captain Chisholm. 'We mustn't take chances with these people.'

The first two men were groaning and beginning to stir, and the Captain examined them. 'Broken jaw here, and –' he paused as he saw how the other lay with eyes half-closed, breathing noisily, 'looks like concussion for this one. I wouldn't be surprised if they both haven't got a broken rib or two, the awkward way they're breathing.' He glanced around. 'We must clear the last three rows of seats for them. Sue, get out the medical chest, will you – and you other first-aiders do all you can for them. I want them watched continually. They weren't very wise, but they did it for all of us.'

Jason looked out of the window once more, then sank back in his seat. No one could cross that stretch of sand unscathed, not the fastest runner. It seemed that there was nothing to be done but to possess themselves in patience, hope that they would soon be discovered and trust that the hijackers' demands be quickly met.

The other passengers were standing up to see better, and there was a hubbub of talk, but a hush fell as Captain Chisholm strode along the gangway and held up his hands for silence.

'We've been hijacked by some pretty determined people,' he said. 'You've all seen what happened to three passengers who tried to take them on. First of all, I want to make it clear that nothing else like this is tried without my express authority. Is that understood?' He looked around and several of the men nodded. 'Now, these people have not identified themselves, and I'm not going to speculate as to which particular group they are. What I can tell you is that I was able to switch on the concealed hijack signal. London should know what has happened to us, though I was unable to report my course or position, as the hijackers saw that I did not use the normal radio transmission system. Now, there are a number of administrative arrangements to be put in hand – '

'Just one minute, Captain.' A slight, middle-aged passenger who had come in from the first-class compartment rose, removing his glasses and tucking them into his breast pocket. 'I presume that the hijackers transmitted certain demands to your control before forbidding you to use your transmission system?' He spoke easily, without fuss or change in expression. 'Just what are these demands, and what reply did you receive?'

'I received no demands to transmit.'

A second passenger jumped up. 'But that's ridiculous! They must have made demands! Otherwise how will we get out of here?' He spoke angrily, in fluent, if accented English. 'And where are we, anyway?' He sat down again, mopping his brow and staring about him as a hubbub of talk broke out again. It died away as Captain Chisholm held up his hand. 'I can't answer your first question, but I can answer the second exactly. We are beached on the east coast of the Pattani province of Thailand, about 46 miles from the north-eastern corner of Malaya.'

'Near Malaya!' This time the hubbub of talk and expostulation was louder, and the Captain held up his hand again. 'Our job is to get organized and make ourselves as comfortable and secure as we can until the civil authorities reach us and arrange our release, as I'm sure they will – '

'I wouldn't bet on it,' muttered the second man, but stopped and looked away as the Captain's eye rested on him.

' – and arrange our release,' he repeated coldly. 'The crew and I will see that certain arrangements are made and we'd be glad of your full co-operation.' Quickly he outlined the need to ration water and food and to organize the use of galley and washrooms, and to regulate sleeping arrangements. Finally he asked the passengers to group themselves by families and languages, for ease of control during possible emergencies. At a pause the first passenger who had spoken commented: 'You seem to have all these arrangements well thought out, Captain.'

Captain Chisholm gave him a swift glance. 'Let's just say that airlines are aware of certain possibilities. Now, I suggest that all those with watches synchronize them to Bangkok time, as that is what the local authorities will use. It is one hour behind Hong Kong time, and I make it now – ' he stood for a moment watching the second hand sweep round – 'twelve twenty-seven exactly.' He waited while watches were adjusted, then went on: 'The next thing is to organize the seating. We may,' he added calmly, 'be here for some time.'

With the injured lying on the three rows of seats nearest the open door, he placed the cabin staff in the next two rows, and then the two children. Seeing Jason watching, he said: 'Were you looking after them?'

'Just reading to them a bit.'

'You O.K. to carry on? It would help a lot.'

'Sure.' Jason nodded. 'I'll stay with them.'

'Good lad!' The Captain moved on, placing the passengers by families in three big groups, with the co-pilot, flight engineer and navigator in charge of one each. That done, he had a word with the senior steward and soon there came sounds of activity from the galley as lunch was prepared.

In the meantime Jason joined the queue for the washrooms, and when his turn arrived he tidied himself and washed his face and hands – only to find that this washroom, the first of the three after washrooms, had run out of paper towels. With his face wet and soapy, water dripping down from his eyebrows, he groped about for the supplies he knew must be kept somewhere in one of the cabinets. With his eyes tight shut, his senses seemed somehow keener, and he noticed a faint yet sharp scent – one he at first assumed to be disinfectant. But what puzzled him as he groped about was its source; it seemed to be percolating through the aircraft bulkhead, and this struck him as ludicrous. Smells didn't penetrate metal! By now he had located the spare tissues and he wiped and dried his face and, his curiosity aroused, examined the wall behind the cabinet. When he put his hand against it he realized that it was not the heavy metal of a bulkhead, but merely thin sheeting covered with a plastic trim of grained leatherette – and the sharp scent drifted in from a barely distinguishable vertical seam, like the join of a panel.

A discreet tap on the door reminded him that he had now been in the washroom for several minutes and that others were waiting. He quickly finished drying his hands and face and left – but that false panel and the unfamiliar sharp scent behind it intrigued him, and he determined to have a closer look at it later on.

It was now very warm inside the aircraft, and the reflected glare from the sea struck in at them through the windows. Jason mopped his face. How long could they go on like this? He returned to his seat to find lunch being wheeled along on trolleys – but this was not the lunch shown on the menu, of fresh prawn hors d'oeuvres with cocktail sauce; noisettes of lamb chasseur with buttered Brussels sprouts and Marquise potatoes, followed by Pêche Condé, cheese, cream crackers, and a choice of coffees.

Instead there was water, soup, biscuits and cheese – and a choice for Hindu and Muslim passengers of chicken or vegetarian dishes. 'Rationing in force, Sir,' said the stewardesses, cheerfully. Jason felt that they were relieved to be busy once more. He helped the children and, like them, finished his soup but could touch nothing else; it was too hot. 'You'd be better off without those shirts,' he said to Margaret, 'and those socks – anything to keep cool.' He helped them out of their clothing and himself stripped off his shirt and sat in his white, sleeveless vest. Then the stewardess brought round and handed to each passenger an elliptical white tablet. 'Salt tablets; please swallow with a sip of water.'

'But this will make me thirsty,' protested one passenger.

'It will relieve your thirst, Sir – it's very important. Salt loss causes heat-stroke.'

'No, no.' The passenger, an Indian, handed it back. 'I do not believe in such patent medicines.' He mopped his face and neck. 'See? I am overheated already!'

With a resigned smile the stewardess moved along and soon reached Jason. 'Give the children half a tablet each – and will you see that they take it? It'll make them feel much better.' It was Sue. 'I've taken mine, I promise you!'

'All right.' Jason took his doubtfully; surely the salt would only increase his thirst! But he swallowed it obediently and, to his surprise, the vague discomfort that had oppressed him for the last half-hour began to disappear. 'Here, you two,' he ordered, 'this'll make you feel better.' He dissolved one tablet in a cup of water and made them drink half each. His surge of relief as the flush on their foreheads began to lessen surprised him; he hadn't realized how concerned he had been for them. Then it struck him how concerned his own parents must be. They'd be worried sick; and the two children's parents, lying injured in hospital in Hong Kong, how would they feel? It was at this moment that he felt his own fears overtaken by anger and by a determination to do something, anything, to help get them all out of this. But what?

3
THE SEA

'IT's stoking up!' The Captain wiped a trickle of sweat from his forehead, looked along the rows of seats where passengers, stripped to their vests, slumped listlessly, fanning themselves with newspapers and menu cards, and got to his feet. 'We've been here long enough for our friends to simmer down and relax a bit.'

The co-pilot looked up at him. 'What are you going to do?'

'Ask them if we can start up the fridge pack.'

The co-pilot looked sceptical. 'They won't let you near it.'

'It's worth a try.' He walked along the gangway forward towards the first-class cabin, pulled aside the curtain and recoiled, the muzzle of an automatic in his face. He began to explain but was thrust back by a rough hand in the chest and the curtain jerked across again.

'Captain – ' One of the Korean passengers hurried along the gangway. 'I can speak some Japanese.'

'Oh, that's wonderful! Will you tell them that all we want is to start up the air-conditioning motor? It'll just be for short periods. We can't run it for long, because of the batteries, but it would help to cool us down.' Captain Chisholm moved aside and the Korean stepped forward and called through the curtain. There was a moment's pause, a muttered discussion, then a curt reply. The Korean shook his head. 'They say No.'

'I was afraid of that. But thank you anyway, Mr – ?'

'Kim, Captain – Kim Chong-sol.'

'Thank you, Mr Kim. Will you translate for me when I speak to them next?'

'Of course.' The Korean bowed and returned to his seat, and Captain Chisholm walked slowly back along the gangway, the passengers looking up at him, some in hope, others in silent resignation. Half-way down he paused, and with a quick 'Excuse me,' leant over a row of seats and pulled the emergency exit handles. One after the other the two oblong windows on the starboard side popped out, struck the wing with a clatter and splashed down into the water. At once the heavy air in the cabin began to move with the through draught, and there were long sighs of relief. 'Don't try jumping out,' he said to the nearest passengers with a dry smile.

With lunch out of the way, the Captain quietly summoned his flight crew and the Senior Steward to a council of war, held in the space between door and galley. Jason, hot and bored, listened without interest as they went over lists of stores on board and discussed the problem of sanitation, ventilation, the run-down of stand-by batteries and other technicalities, but his ears pricked up when he heard the words ' – Coast,' and 'Kra Ishmus'.

'. . . over this way years ago, on the Singapore–Bangkok run,' the Captain was saying. 'I've never met anyone yet who's actually set foot on this strip of coast. We always reckoned there was nothing down here but elephants and aborigines.'

'There must be fishing villages, Skipper.'

'Oh, yes, here and there along the coast.'

'If one of us could get past these blokes,' said the navigator, 'it'd be easy walking along the beach. There must be a fishing village along here somewhere!' He lowered his voice and Jason strained to hear. 'There are the two starboard emergency exits. One of us could get out and along the wing, maybe get past them that way.'

'That'd be the same as jumping down from the passenger door. As soon as you hit the sand they'd fill you in. No,' and Captain Chisholm shook his head, 'I'm not sending anyone out to get shot.'

'If we don't get help soon that big chap's going to die. Anyway – why hide us away down here? Hijackers like the world to watch!'

'Perhaps they're making the world sweat first,' said Captain Chisholm. 'Pity we can't use our set, even to listen.' He looked out of the door. 'At least they don't seem to be very successful. They've moved their set away from the wing, and they're swinging the aerial about, trying to get a better signal.'

'It's that big ridge to the west,' said the Flight Engineer. 'They won't get distant stations down in this pocket without a decent aerial – not from that direction anyhow. They should get local stations easily enough, though, KL and Bangkok.'

'These stations don't broadcast in Japanese!'

'Well, they're pointing the wrong way for Tokyo. Pity we haven't a set ourselves; at least we'd hear the news.'

At that something flashed across Jason's mind, something he'd seen – he remembered, and pulled himself up in his seat. 'Captain! – ' and he waved his hand.

The Captain looked round, eyebrows raised, and Jason, awkward at first, stammered: 'There is a set – one of the passengers has a handbag transistor! I saw it when we were being searched!' He pointed to the Chinese lady.

'Good for you.' Captain Chisholm hurried along the gangway. 'I believe you may have a transistor radio, Madam?'

She looked up in surprise, then gave a deprecating smile, 'I have one here, but it is not working.' She took the little oblong case from her bag. 'Always it worked very nicely, but now it gives nothing but crackling.'

'May I borrow it?'

'Certainly.' She handed it to him, and he walked swiftly back with it.

'Here you are, Tim.' He handed it to the Flight Engineer. 'Try it.'

'Let's see.' The Flight Engineer switched on and listened to the buzz and crackle as he moved the tuning knob along the medium-wave band. 'Batteries O.K., but aerial interference heavy. It's the fuselage all round us; the set just needs earthing properly.' He searched his pockets, then turned to the others: 'Any of you got a bit of copper wire handy? No?' He looked around. 'Perhaps the galley . . . I've got it! Sue – got a hairpin?'

'I think so.' She took down her bag in its airline colours,

searched through it and produced a paper packet. 'Have a dozen!'

'No thanks, just one.' He took a hairpin, straightened it out, stuck one end into the radio's earth socket and pushed the other against the nearest metal window-casing. At once the crackle of static vanished. He turned the dial along gently, and loud and clear came a woman's voice – nasal Chinese, punctuated by the clash of cymbals and the squeal of bamboo pipes. 'Chinese opera! That won't tell us much!' He turned the dial further, passed a jumble of voices: the rapid mutter of Tamil; Malay, sonorous and impressive; other incomprehensible languages – and suddenly, English!

'Wheesht!' He adjusted the tuning knob delicately. 'It's a weather forecast – with luck there'll be the news in a minute.' They listened with strained attention.

'. . . clearing from the north-east. Some turbulence, however, is expected in the wake of Typhoon Agnes which has now turned south just short of Hong Kong.' 'At least we're clear of that lot!' muttered the navigator.

'Listen!' grunted the Captain.

They waited impatiently as the weather reports ended and news of forthcoming programmes was announced, the stewardesses silent, and Jason hanging over the back of his seat. At last there came the first four notes of the Malaysian national anthem, 'Terang Bulan', and a voice announcing in good English: 'Radio Malaysia.' The news began, not as they had hoped with reports of themselves but of storm damage in Taiwan caused by Typhoon Agnes and of concern for ships in the South China Sea. They listened impatiently while he spoke of storm warnings, then held their breaths as he went on: 'It is not thought that the missing airliner bound from Hong Kong to Bangkok had been affected in any way by the typhoon. Airline officials confirmed that initial signals had been received indicating that hijackers were on board, but no news has been received of a landing at any airport. Our air correspondent points out that without refuelling the aircraft must land by mid-afternoon.' No one spoke or looked up; all around stood intently listening.

'Our London correspondent states that there is as yet no confirmation of reports that the airline has received a demand, delivered anonymously to the head office, that six named liberation fighters held by Israel must be freed before the aircraft and passengers are released. Unofficial sources in the British Foreign and Commonwealth Office indicate that a similar demand had been received there in the early hours of the morning, that is, after the aircraft had taken off from Hong Kong, and that it had been signed by Rengo Sekigun, the Japanese so-called United Red Army. An air and sea search is being made and ships in the Gulf of Siam have been requested to look out for the aircraft or survivors. Now here are some items of local news. The visit to Segamat by the Yang di-Pertuan Agong to mark the opening of the new timber and pulp-mill at Batu Hitam – '

'So that's it.' Captain Chisholm switched off. 'We're to be used to put pressure on Israel.'

'Rengo Sekigun, eh?' The co-pilot made a face. 'That's the suicide gang that did the Lod Airport massacre in June '72.'

' 'Fraid so – and we all know Israel's attitude to hijack demands.'

'But why hide us away down here?' the navigator broke in. 'Surely, now that the news has broken, they'd let us signal our position!'

'I think I know why – and why they're so busy with their set out there.' Captain Chisholm looked thoughtful. 'They know we'll be located sooner or later – even down here a VC 10 on the beach is pretty obvious. No, they're listening for something, and until they hear it, we can sit in this aircraft till we rot.'

'And the wounded?'

'The same. Now, go off to your groups and pass on what we've heard – but make it as matter-of-fact as you can; there's no use in causing alarm.'

Even with the faint breeze through the emergency hatches the heat inside the stranded aircraft was now very great. Beside Jason the children slept fitfully, exhausted. A fly or two buzzed in through the open door and Jason, for want of anything better to do, watched the lethargic blows at them as they zoomed among the passengers' heads. His earlier hopes of speedy release had long been dashed. At first he had been irritated by the thought that their release might not come soon enough for his heats on Saturday, but he now saw that as trivial. The stony, hostile faces of the hijackers, the wounded lying two rows behind him, the explosive carefully wired to the fuel tanks – all made him realize the stark truth: they were held by ruthless killers. He looked down at the children again, hoping that his own fear would not transmit itself to them.

A hot hour dragged past, and for something to do he joined the queue to the washrooms again. He could have another look at that panel. It probably opened into a bit of the works, but at least he could find out. When his turn came, he found himself opposite one of the other two washrooms. Quickly he said to the man behind him: 'I'll wait for this other one – I think I left my handkerchief in it earlier,' and moved aside to let him pass. To his relief no one seemed to think this unusual, and when his turn came, he slipped inside and made straight for the false panel. He ran his hands up and down the crack, felt a catch and pulled, gently at first, then harder. It clicked open and he stared in.

He was looking into a big chamber as tall as himself, with a metal storage tank on one side from which branched out a maze of stainless steel pipes, beneath them a shallow drip tray holding a thin film of liquid from which faint vapour fumes arose. Jason guessed that the chamber was something to do with the hydraulic system. The gleaming maze of pipes, the mysterious storage tank and the peculiar fumes had a menacing air about them which made him uneasy, and he was about to close the panel when he realized that the weak light in the chamber did not all come from behind him. Jason stared harder. The far metal bulkhead behind did not go all the way down. What had looked like a shadowy extension of it was, in fact, an opening into a larger compartment below. He could only see into a corner of it, but made out a heap of bundles with among them, unmistakably, a suitcase. He was looking down into a corner of the after luggage bay, and the door must have been left ajar by the hijackers. Again he heard impatient queuers tapping, but for the moment ignored them while he ran his eye over the space in front of him and paused once more. The pipes did not go quite up to the ceiling. There might just be room ... Again came the impatient taps, louder and more insistent this time. 'Coming,' he called, clicked back the panel and slipped out with a murmured apology.

He walked slowly back, deep in thought – but, as he passed the rear door, he glanced out and his vision of himself climbing down into the luggage bay and running for help evaporated like smoke. The two hijackers, automatics slung, squatted cross-legged under the port wing. In daylight he would be seized the moment he dropped to the sand, and even in darkness he would be heard and, very likely, be caught by a burst of automatic fire.

He felt the aircraft jerk and quiver, and grabbed at his seat. Others had felt the same, and one man, squinting down through the glass of a starboard window, called: 'The tide's coming in – the undercarriage is sinking into the wet sand!' The aircraft gave another lurch, no more

43

than an inch or two, but the stressed metal skin vibrated. Jason ignored it for he was up in his seat trying to stare down through the window, and he caught a glimpse of a faint line of foam, wave by wave, washing further up the beach. The sea, he thought – he'd forgotten the sea !

'They're up to something, Captain!' The steward on watch called round the corner of the galley and Captain Chisholm sprang for the door. A third hijacker had appeared below the wing, and with the other two was examining the transistor radio set. 'Looks as if they're not getting any results. Pity they're a bit too far off for Mr Kim to hear what they're saying.' He watched as they realigned the aerial and adjusted the tuning. 'Hullo!' One of the hijackers had snapped down the extended aerial and the third man picked it up. 'They're moving it!'

'Look's as if he's taking it up to the flight deck, Sir !'

'I think you're right. They can't have been getting any results under that wing.' Thoughtful, he moved back and to his place, and he was discussing the possible significance of the Japanese hijackers' action when there was an unexpected interruption.

'You! Come!'

At the sharp command in English the dozing, sweating passengers looked up. In the doorway of the first-class cabin stood a hijacker with an automatic in his right hand, his left pointing at Captain Chisholm. 'Come!' he repeated.

'Maybe something's happening – they may have news!' Captain Chisholm jumped from his seat and hurried along the gangway. The hijacker jammed the automatic against his back as he passed through, and, as the curtain swung to behind them, a buzz of speculation broke out among the passengers. 'It may be news about their demands!' cried one hopefully.

'Too soon for that,' grunted another. 'But they might let us stretch our legs.'

'These hijackers'll have to do something about the injured.' The first-class passenger with the heavy glasses, stripped to his waist but still imperturbable, spoke quietly. 'And there are older people here whose hearts aren't too good.' For some moments the discussion and speculation kept up, but soon died away. It was too hot for the effort of coherent thought.

'We could do with one of these tropical rainstorms — that would cool this thing down,' said another passenger fanning himself with the map showing his route to England. 'I thought this area was supposed to have rain every day.'

'Doesn't look much like it now.' Others near him looked out of the windows at the sea. 'There's a flat calm.'

'It's oppressive — there's not a breath of air. Perhaps we'll get some rain tonight.'

'Here's the Captain again!' All heads lifted as the curtain parted, but they saw only his back; he seemed to be standing arguing with someone beyond. 'He's taking a bit of a chance,' muttered someone; then *crack* came the sound of the butt of an automatic striking flesh and bone, the Captain's head jerked round with the force of the blow and he toppled backwards along the gangway, legs, shoulders and head hitting the deck at the same moment.

'Captain!' The nearest passenger sprang down to help him, but he lay absolutely still. 'They've killed him!'

'Here, let me see.' The co-pilot forced his way past the craning heads and shoulders and knelt by the man on the floor. 'Still breathing.' He waved to the Flight Engineer: 'Tim, take his head.' Lifting the Captain by head and legs, they staggered aft along the gangway and laid him along the crew's row of seats. A red weal showed the oval imprint of the butt across the swelling side of his face and jaw and blood ran from his nose. 'Just as well he hit carpet, or he'd have fractured his skull.' The co-pilot ran his hands over the unconscious man's head and face. 'He's only knocked out. Get his shoes off – that's it – and lift his feet up a bit higher than his head.'

'Here.' Sue appeared with cotton-wool and disinfectant. 'I'll clean that up a bit.' She worked efficiently, and, while she was applying ointment to the battered face, the Captain groaned and moved his head.

'Don't move, Captain.' The co-pilot put a restraining hand on his shoulder. 'Just take it easy, everything's under control.'

'Hullo.' Captain Chisholm opened his eyes and shut them again. 'What happened?'

'One of those Japs fetched you one with a gun-butt. But don't worry about it now, just rest.'

To Jason, listening and looking on, it seemed as if he was watching a series of disconnected incidents in a rather bad but very violent film – one in which he might at any moment find himself taking part. But the Captain was speaking again. 'Asked for the women and children to be let out into the shade.' He spoke thickly. 'Bitten my tongue.'

'What did they call you for first, though?' the co-pilot asked. 'Anything about the demands?'

The Captain answered without moving or opening his eyes. 'Set trouble. I showed them the earth socket.' He lay a moment, breathing in short painful gasps through one side of his mouth. 'Got it loud and clear.'

'What station, Captain?' Tim leant close to him. 'Did you see the frequency?'

'They shoved me out.' His eyes were still closed. 'Shoved me out.'

The others looked up at each other; he was beginning to wander. The co-pilot looked grim: this vagueness after an initial few moments of clarity was often a sign of concussion. 'Just take it easy.'

Captain Chisholm put a hand up to his face and said in a thick mumble: 'Arabic, couldn't understand a word.'

'He means Japanese,' said the co-pilot. He was talking nonsense, all right. 'Don't worry, Captain – lie still.' He signalled for a cushion to be put under the injured man's head. 'You'll feel better if you get some sleep. Think you'll manage?'

The Captain mumbled something in a drowsy voice and the co-pilot got up. 'Keep a close eye on him,' he said in a low voice. 'He's concussed, all right. How are the other three?'

The second stewardess shook her head slightly. 'Two are half awake, but this one' – and she indicated the big man with the scalpel wound – 'looks very bad. I don't like his colour, he can't speak or move, and there's still some bleeding.'

The senior steward got up and caught his eye. 'I think everyone'd be better for a cup of tea, Sir.'

'Good idea.'

In a few minutes the stewardesses were wheeling their trolleys along the gangway. 'Tea for the adults, soft drinks for the children. Margaret, John – lemon or orange?' The children stirred from their heavy sleep, flushed, sweaty and at first bewildered. They soon sat up, but, as Jason helped them with their drinks, he saw how their small bodies were showing the first rash of prickly heat. Sue brought him a damp flannel and a tin of powder. 'Sponge them down and put on a light dusting of this. It'll help. Get them to change positions every so often, it'll stop them getting too cramped.'

'When are we going home?' asked Margaret. From her face Jason saw that she sensed the change in the mood of heightened tension in their prison.

'Soon,' he reassured her, 'but we'll have to sleep here, tonight. I'll read you something now. Sue,' he called, 'is there another book? I've finished this one.'

But the little girl cried out: 'Tigers again!' and at his quick look of surprise laughed, and her brother obediently laughed as well. 'Tigers!' he echoed.

'All right!' Patiently Jason began to read, and, as he watched the children gradually settle back in their seats and relax, he realized that they liked hearing the same story – it was familiar, the characters were kindly and, above all, there was a happy ending. Some instinct told them that there was no guarantee of a happy ending to their present plight.

So Jason read and the children listened; then, as the afternoon wore on, a sudden breeze sprang up and there were murmurs and gasps of relief all round him. The sun was now well over to the west, the bright glare from the water vanished and the sea – no longer a sheet of metal shining into their eyes – was blue again, flurried by the breeze and, to Jason, more enticing than ever.

With the growing cool the hours to evening passed more easily, and a cold supper was brought round early, to catch the last of the fading light. Jason, restless and unsettled, did little more than pick at the slice of cold luncheon meat and rye-bread that was his ration of supper, though the children ate theirs with relish. His mind was beginning to stray back to that chamber behind the panel and to the sea outside. The tide was well in: when he stood up he saw the water close up to the line of seaweed and flotsam of the high-water mark; the hijackers on the beach had moved further up and now sat under the far end of the great wing. The one disguised as a woman had now changed into men's clothing, and Jason wondered, as he looked at that sullen face with its strong jaw and cropped hair, how he could ever have passed for a woman, even with rouge, lipstick and a kimono.

Just out of curiosity he began to calculate the depth of water in which Speedwing II stood. When they had splashed down the undercarriage had stood in little more than a few inches of water, for the hijackers, only a little way up the beach, had sat on dry sand. Some tides, he knew, were enormous – in one place in the Channel tides had been known of nearly thirty feet. This wouldn't have applied here, though: they were in the tropics, near the Equator, where tides were less extreme. No, the tides would be small – only seven or eight feet. If that were so, he thought with quickened interest, there was probably six feet of water below them at this moment.

Beside him the children were drowsing again. 'Here, you two.' It was Sue with a sheet. 'Time for bed.' She reclined the seats, pushing down the arm-rests between them, and covered the children up.

'I'll get back to my own place,' whispered Jason. 'Good night, Margaret, good night, John. Sleep well!' He crossed to his seat next to the big Chinese. They chatted desultorily but soon fell silent. Everyone was weary – exhausted by the early departure from Hong Kong and the long day of tension and heat. This was nothing like a conventional hijacking, with its glare of floodlights, the TV cameras and thronging journalists, the officials bargaining, threatening, surrendering – here there was only an empty shore, the outline of a forested ridge against the night sky and silence, except for the lap of the sea.

A single emergency bulb came on in the cabin and suddenly everything outside was dark. Jason got up restlessly and walked along the gangway. Most people were back in their seats and, for the first time for hours, there was no queue for the washrooms. He paused by the injured. Two, he saw, lay with their eyes open; the Captain was apparently asleep, but the man with the stab wound was ominously quiet and Jason knew he must be very near death. One man kept watch over the injured and another sat by the door. The others of the crew sprawled asleep. Occasionally a powerful torch flashed out from the beach, its beam lighting up the fuselage and throwing quick shadows across the sleepers inside, then turning down on the surface of the sea before being switched off.

A wild thought was forming in Jason's mind. He tried to shut it out, but it kept returning. He wandered back along the gangway in the dim light of the bulb, glanced down at the sleeping children and then back to the injured. He turned and walked aft to the first washroom. It was vacant. He went inside and stood for a moment, trying to control his unsteady breathing. Someone had to get help. The hijackers would be bound to miss one of the crew, but not a passenger — and he could swim. *He* must go. He felt for the catch and pulled open the concealed panel. The faint light from the washroom glimmered on the steel pipes and again he sensed that menacing scent. He hesitated, then quickly pushed himself through the opening and into the chamber beyond. He groped for the pipes, found a box-like projection in the bulkhead and stood on it, reaching up to gauge the width between the ceiling and the top of the pipes. He might just do it. He pulled himself up, shutting his eyes tight to keep out the sting of the fumes, reached the top of the clustering pipes and wriggled across, thanking his stars that they were smooth, slippery almost. Then with a heave he was over and tumbling down into the luggage bay. For a moment or two he lay sprawled among the suitcases and packages, wondering whether he had done himself any damage in his fall, but he felt nothing worse than a banged shin. At least he'd made little noise.

He looked for the door — and had a quick moment of

terror when he saw only darkness. Had the hijackers shut it again? He felt his way across the luggage bay till he touched the metal fuselage. Groping along it, he came to a crack, it widened at his touch and he saw a star. He pushed, the door moved silently back, he looked down and saw the gleam of water.

The torch beam shone out, flickered over the fuselage and down to the sea and Jason ducked back – but he was safe in the belly of the aircraft, and that torchlight beam had shown him the surface of the water, no more than five feet below him. He slipped off his shoes, tied the laces together and hung the shoes round his neck, turned and lowered himself backwards till he was propped by his fore-arms. He swung his foot but still could not feel the water. He was gasping with apprehension. He was being too slow, but if he just let go the splash would alert that hijacker with the torch. He tried to lower himself by his hands, but there was nothing to grasp, only the smooth metal of the door, and it was moving, sliding away as he grabbed it.

The torch shone out on the fuselage above him. Jason grabbed for a handhold to pull himself up before the beam swept down and caught his dangling legs, but his hand slipped and he fell with a heavy splash into the sea.

4

THE FOREST

JASON twisted in the water, with one stroke pulled himself down to the sandy bottom and glanced back up at the surface. The broken foam of his fall gleamed greeny-white in the torch beam, and the widening ring of waves was suddenly cut by a line of small splashes. Like a flash he turned and swam along the bottom and surfaced with barely a ripple behind one of the huge wheels of the undercarriage. He clung to it, gulping in air in long deep breaths, methodically filling his lungs fuller and fuller. He had lost the shoes round his neck in the fall but did not give them a second thought; his first concern was to get away out to sea without being shot.

The torch beam flickered wildly across the water, trying to locate him; he heard a voice in Japanese, it seemed to be calling from high up, from the nose of the aircraft; there was an answering shout of *'Hai!'* and then the splashes of someone running into the shallows and hitting the surface in a flat racing dive. Jason took a last long breath, sank beneath the surface, put both feet against the great tyre and pushed hard. He shot along the sea-bed like an otter, feet and hands working rhythmically, angling away from the aircraft and out to his left, towards the rocky promontory sticking out into the sea at the far end of the beach.

Just before his breath gave out, he slowed down, let himself drift to the surface and looked back. Sixty yards behind him the great aircraft bulked high against the trees. He trod water for a moment, blinking sea-water from his eyes and taking long deep breaths. He was clear. He floated, letting his heart-thumps subside when he saw something which set his blood racing again. Against the metal of the fuselage a small dark blob appeared outlined on the water. It vanished and reappeared, this time rather closer to him. He dashed the water from his eyes and stared harder. It was a head. Whoever it was who had done that racing dive into the sea had seen him, and was turning towards him.

Jason turned and set off at a fast crawl. He had to get distance between himself and his pursuer; time enough to wear him out later – first he had to get clear. He swam confidently – he'd show this fellow! Fifty yards on, he paused in his stroke to look back, and felt a shock of surprise. The round dark blob was nearer. Though still huge on the beach the aircraft seemed suddenly remote, the stretch of dark water between might have been a hundred miles instead of a hundred yards. Jason began thrashing through the water, swimming clumsily and panting with effort, till he took a deep breath and forced himself to settle into a better stroke.

He changed direction once more, not towards the promontory beyond the aircraft but away from it, hoping that in the darkness and by swimming with little splash he'd shake off his pursuer, but a quick glance back showed that dark blob turning to follow. It was uncanny. He felt the first stab of despair and had to check himself from thrashing out wildly again, and then he realized: his vest – he still wore his white vest!

He turned back towards the promontory, swimming furiously and with that head turning to follow him, but with every third or fourth stroke Jason snatched at his vest, pulling it farther and farther up till it was up round his shoulders. At last he got an arm out; then, slowing down a moment, dragged the vest over his head. Leaving it floating, a pale patch on the water, he dived away from it and turned again, straight out to sea. A safe distance away he surfaced, lungs bursting and arms trembling with strain. The vest still floated, but he caught the brief swirl of churned water beyond it, moving away from him towards the rocky promontory.

For a long moment he floated, then set off at an easy breaststroke. He swam steadily now, with no more fear of pursuit, his one idea to put as much distance between himself and the hijackers as possible. When well out he turned and swam parallel with the shore. The moon's rim was just appearing directly to his right as he swam, a moon just past the full, and as it rose and its light increased he made out the rocks, about three hundred yards inshore of him. He was tempted to drift ashore – how inviting they looked, the lap and gurgle of the tide against them!

Fear and prudence conquered his fatigue; he swam on, seeing another beach, the image of the one which held the aircraft – another long, anonymous beach. The tide was still on the make. At last he let himself drift in, eyes just above the surface. The long sweep of pale sand was empty. Beyond it the trees were in total darkness. He drifted in till his knees trailed against sand. He rested in the shallows, only the top of his head above the water, then after some minutes stood up and dashed for the line of trees. He tripped over a fallen palm frond in the dark, rolled over, pushed himself up, found he was on short grass, turned and hurried stumbling along it and slithered into a shallow depression, between tufts of coarse grass and bushes. The dense forest was still twenty yards away but here he was within the palm line, in black shadow. In the depression the surface of the sand was dew-damp and chilly, but, underneath, it still bore the sun's warmth.

Hastily he scraped a place for himself, got in and swept the warm sand over him. Almost before his head fell back, he was asleep.

Some time after midnight the cold woke him. After the first hours of heavy, almost drugged sleep he stirred, trying to scrape himself down deeper into the sand but eventually, shivering, opened his eyes to see palm fronds above him, black and silver in the moonlight. A breeze set the leaves rattling and he huddled down into the sand again, trying as best he could to pile it against his bare chest. His trousers had dried on him, and he took them off, wrapped them round his chest and shoulders and lay shivering and longing for dawn and the sun. At last grey light showed up the dark boles of the palms. It paled and strengthened, the clouds glowed pink then brilliant white, and as the sun rose the sea turned from grey to blue.

He blinked around sleepily. Now was the time for a good rest, in the warmth of the sun. He glanced idly out to sea and sat up sharply. There was a fishing boat out there, its square sail up and its painted prow shining. That would be better than walking along goodness knows how many beaches! He'd run out and wave to it. He brushed the sand from his chest and ribs, pulled on his trousers, stepped up from the sand hollow – and flung himself down again. A man with cropped black hair was walking briskly along the fringe of seaweed marking the high-water mark, a short, stocky man in shirt and trousers, a sub-machine-gun slung under one arm.

Jason looked at the forest behind. The short grass under the palms ended at a head-high green wall of huge, rhodo-dendron-like bushes with pale green leaves, and behind this wall the forest trees stood up. If he made a dash for those trees he'd be seen. He lay flat against the hollow, peering between the clumps of short coarse grass at the man striding out along the beach. He looked neither to his right, out to sea, nor to his left, towards the palms and the forest, and Jason gradually felt his fright subside. The hijacker would simply walk on below him, and once he was well past, Jason could slip back into the trees – or even stay hidden in this same little hollow in the sand; it was well concealed and pleasantly warm now that the sun was up, though later it might well get too hot for comfort. That Jap could walk on till he dropped!

The hijacker was closer now, and Jason saw beneath the flapping shirt the bulge of chest and shoulder muscles, the smooth and heavy muscles of a swimmer, and last night's fear seized him again. Still the Japanese strode briskly along, looking to neither right nor left and keeping to the high-water mark. He was closer now, not much more than a hundred yards away, and as he walked he scrutinized the sand just ahead of him. Jason felt his heart lurch in his chest. Below him his footprints led up from the sea straight to the hollow where he lay.

Jason turned and crawled from the sand-hollow, keeping flat between the clumps of coarse grass. His back muscles twitched as he moved, but he reached the fringe of bushes undetected, began forcing himself through beneath the lowest branches – and found himself caught in a tangle of springy stems. He felt forward into the tangle, found a main trunk and started to pull himself through, but the rubbery stems, like bundles of thin arms, seemed to stretch out to hold him.

Terrified of shaking the leaves and giving himself away, he paused and, very cautiously, turned his head and looked over his shoulder at the Japanese, now nearly directly below him. As Jason watched, his pace quickened and he ran forward, bent to examine the sand, straightened up, turned and walked quickly up towards the palm line, unslinging his automatic as he came.

Jason pulled himself forward. A branch caught on the

waistband of his trousers, the bush twitched, he heard a shout, he heaved with both arms and thrust with his feet, there was another shouted command, he heaved again and burst through the clutching stems and rolled among tree-ferns. He bounded up, scuttled on all fours through the thicker undergrowth, and once among the tall trees got up and ran for his life.

He ran wildly, zig-zagging, leaping exposed tree-roots, stumbling and running on again, his ears straining backwards for sounds of pursuit. The level ground sloped upwards, he began to slow down and turned and raced along the foot of the slope. He had covered a good eighty yards before he heard the crash and rattle of something forcing through the same hedge of bushes, and the sound galvanized him: he must hide, he couldn't keep running, he'd be heard – and his bare feet stung and ached. He slowed to a trot, panting and trying to see on through the trees. A big white tree with buttresses at its base was just ahead of him, and he half-fell, half-scrambled round behind it and crouched between two of the growing supports. He drew a shuddering breath; the buttresses hid him but he felt vulnerable – this great tree was too obvious. He slipped away from it, risked a glance back, saw thorn fronds jerk and shake, scuttled to one side and flung himself flat behind one of the scatter of fallen and rotted branches on the ground.

Jason heard the pad-scrape, pad-scrape of trotting feet across the slope till they were just above him. They paused by the big tree, he pressed his face closer down against the earth, he heard the feet again, they padded on and he lay, hardly daring to breathe, till the sound died away. At last he raised his head and lay listening. He caught a distant sound, then silence. He turned and, crouching low, set off at a run up the slope and deeper into the forest.

After the first moments Jason realized the slope was

steepening, and he slowed down, gulping and looking about for an easier way of escape. He turned to his right across the slope but found this even more difficult, with the soft crumbly humus breaking away from his feet, so turned and ran uphill till at last he stopped and sank to the ground, his breath coming in great shuddering gasps and his leg muscles twitching with effort. He crouched on the ground, head hanging while gradually his breathing steadied, then wiped the sweat from his eyebrows and looked about him.

All around were tall, straight forest trees, crowding in on each other so that, whichever way he looked, he saw only columns of trunks reaching up to the sky, itself hidden by the tree-tops, all intermingled to form a dense roof high above. From it, he heard bird calls, but down on the forest floor there was stillness and quiet. If he too stayed quiet no one would ever find him.

He stood up, felt stabs of pain from both feet, sat down again and looked at them. Long shallow cuts criss-crossed his ankles, cuts as fine as if made by a razor-blade, and his soles were studded with small black dots, and when he touched one, the pain made him flinch. He had to examine them carefully, running his fingers gingerly across the hard skin before he realized what these were – snapped-off thorn spines. He tried to pull some of them out but soon saw that he needed tweezers. Some spines were deeply embedded, but these were clustered in the balls of his feet, on which he had run. His heels and the sides of his feet had escaped. He got up and stood listening. There was no sound, no leaf moved, he heard no footstep. Had that Japanese gone back to the aircraft? But he also listened for what he did not hear – the sound of a helicopter, or perhaps a motor boat. Rescue was still far off. There was nothing for it: he would have to circle as best he could, get back to the beach again and make for a village; he'd never find his way through this forest. He set off up the slope, placing his feet with care and pausing every few minutes to listen. He now saw that he was on a distinct, rising spur, and guessed that it led up to the ridge he had seen from the aircraft. In half an hour he reached a point where the slope levelled out, and then he heard running water, and at that faint sound he realized how thirsty he was.

The stream was a few yards in front of him, and he was about to move forward to it and drink when his eye was caught by a broad leaf lying on the ground. In direct contrast to the brown humus underfoot this leaf was fresh and green. He picked it up. The stem had been sliced through, and, as he held it, a drop of sap oozed out. He looked across the stream, saw nothing and moved forward, walking carefully on his painful feet. Whoever else was about, he must have water; his tongue seemed coated with the salt of the sea and he was pouring with sweat from his uphill run. He knelt to drink, but paused at a slight sound, a steady series of clicks and rustles and low voices. There was movement across the stream; he made out an arm, then a small brown body, not quite naked, no more than twenty paces beyond. He stared. Suddenly, like a puzzle that resolves into a picture when looked at long enough, the crowding confusion of trunks and leaves and twigs and fronds seemed to open to reveal half a dozen lean-to shelters, partially thatched, with a number of small brown people busily plaiting leaves watched by a greybeard smoking a tiny pipe.

Keeping his eyes on the people ahead, Jason crouched and began to crawl forward towards the stream – but his movement was caught, he heard an urgent call of warning, a high rolling guttural, the brown figures sprang up and Jason turned and blundered his way back as fast as he could limp and run. He crashed back between the trees, an arm up to shield his face, and ran till the pain slowed him to a limping trot and finally to a halt. He hobbled to the far side of a tree and leant against it, his chest heaving with a mixture of fright and effort. He wiped his face again, feeling, as he did so, the scrape of thorn-stubs. He looked at his hand. More long scratches striped the backs of his knuckles, and the edges of his palms were studded with the dot-like stumps of thorn spines, caught and snapped in his flight.

He began to feel a sense of despair. Here he stood, the forest silent and apparently empty, yet, however much he tried to circle round to the beach again, he seemed to finish up deeper and deeper among the trees, and always pierced by thorns. Then it came to him that he had heard no sounds of pursuit, no thud of running feet behind him nor any warlike cries. He listened, peered about as best he could, and gradually it came to him that whoever they were whom he had stumbled upon, they were as frightened as he was.

He felt a warm surge of relief, and wondered wryly what sort of apparition he must have presented. His fashionably long hair hung in a thick brown tangle, his bare chest, white from a sunless English winter, was striped with blood, and certainly he must have seemed a giant to the little people he had disturbed. He only hoped they wouldn't run into the hijacker.

His watch still ticked, he looked at it and blessed its watertight steel case. It was barely half past eight in the morning, and as his apprehension ebbed, he thought of breakfast. Phrases from that airline menu sprang unbidden into his mind – rolls, butter, ham, eggs, coffee, marmalade . . . But most of all he was thirsty, and he remembered the tiny stream.

He must have water. Jason turned and went back very slowly and painfully the way he had come. He hadn't run very far before going to ground behind that tree. His feet and the difficulty of entangling bushes, tree-roots, fallen branches and the endless stretches of thorn fronds all made a hundred yards seem like a thousand. He was soon back at the little stream. Listening carefully he waited, heard nothing, knelt and drank, gulping down water until his thirst was slaked and he felt uncomfortably full. All the time he was alert for the slightest sound, and when he had finished drinking he backed away from the stream and sat huddled up and straining his ears.

Hunger and curiosity overcame his fear. He could now see the disturbance in the forest pattern made by the little huts, how they provided an artificial sequence of form and shape. There was no one about; he had a feeling of complete solitude. He stood up and hobbled forward.

The little huts, no more than frame lean-tos thatched with leaves, were empty. A small fire smouldered on a bare patch in the centre and he looked eagerly for signs of food – hoping for a cooking-pot containing rice or possibly potatoes, but there was nothing but scraps of what looked like the fur of a squirrel, a cut stick, a skewer of bamboo with a charred end and some unknown vegetable scrapings. One after the other he searched the huts, crouching to peer inside and rummaging through the heaps of leaves. He found nothing. The ends of the cut poles were still pale, the leaves still green and the earth round the cooking fire still soft. The little aborigines had just arrived and had been building a new camp when he had disturbed them. On the ground lay evidence of hasty and immediate flight – a half-finished bit of thatch made from palmetto leaves sliced into parallel strips, folded over each other, a plaited basket – even the greybeard's pipe of carved wood, tobacco ash still warm in the tiny bowl.

Even though he knew he was still alone, he felt uncomfortable standing in the little half-ring of huts.

Instinctively he felt a need to get into the anonymity of the trees, and he was hobbling carefully off when his eye fell on what looked like a longer pole than the others, propped against one of the lean-tos. It was not greyish, like the framework poles, but a smooth, leathery brown, absolutely straight and with a distinct cone-shaped enlargement at one end. It was not till he took it that he realized that it was a blowpipe. Intrigued he put an eye to one end and saw how the bore ran down through it, straight as a gun-barrel and about the width of a cigarette. He hefted it in one hand. It was light, and made not from wood but from cane. The cone at one end was the mouthpiece, rather like a thicker version of the mouthpiece of a trumpet. He held it, thinking. Here was a weapon, not much, but something . . . but he put it down again; not only would it be stealing to take it, it would be just an encumbrance. He was moving slowly enough without carrying blowpipes about. But there was that little cylindrical basket on the ground nearby, a tiny thing, like a child's toy. He picked it up. It was beautifully plaited from thin strips of cane. It wasn't empty, as he had first thought; it held what looked from the open end like little stubs of tightly rolled paper. Gently he pulled one out, taking it delicately with the nails of finger and thumb. The white stub was pith, tightly rolled round the end of a slender skewer of bamboo some eight inches long. It had been carefully nicked two inches from the point, and below the nick the skewer was caked with some dark brown substance. Holding it carefully by the pith end he sniffed at the point. It gave off a strong, narcotic odour, and he saw that it was still sticky. He knew what it was: he remembered his father reminiscing about Malaya and Borneo, talking about aborigines and their blowpipes and darts – poisoned darts . . .

Jason held the dart gingerly away from him by finger

and thumb, conquering his first impulse to fling it into the trees; some barefoot aborigine might tread on it. He looked at the plaited quiver with mistrust, and then the blowpipe caught his eye. He leant over and slid the dart down into it, and the wad of white pith settled snugly into the mouthpiece. There, that was safer – and when the owner returned he'd soon spot it. Carefully Jason stood the blowpipe against the lean-to then walked back to the stream and sat down to think.

It was warm now in the forest, and he no longer felt chilly discomfort from his bare skin. With his thirst quenched, his one overpowering urge was to get help for the people in the aircraft. He *had* to get to a fishing village. The quickest way back down to the shore and that concealing line of palms was straight down the spur again; any other way he might get lost and wander for hours. That hijacker would be back at the plane by now. Jason set off, finding now that he knew more or less where he was heading, that movement in the forest was easier than he had expected. He was more than half-way back to the beach and gaining confidence with every step when he saw the jerk and quiver of fronds shaking, some way below. He froze. A cropped head turned up towards him, he saw the quick look of recognition and turned and ran.

Sore feet forgotten, Jason raced uphill. Leaves crashed as the hijacker thrust his way up on to the spur and Jason heard the thud of his feet pounding behind. Faintly through the tree-tops drifted another sound, the distant beat of an engine, but to Jason it meant nothing – he knew only that his hunter followed, and he himself was weakening.

He paused a moment for breath, gasping and crowing, heard running feet and forced himself on, but he knew he was being overtaken. Then it came to him: the camp – he could hide in the camp! He was still just out of sight of the man behind. Jason put on a spurt, then turned away from the spur, ran through the trees to the little stream and plunged across it, and at little more than a trot stumbled into the camp. He could run no more.

He walked a pace or two, gulping for breath, blinking sweat from his eyes, trying to regain control of his shaking thigh muscles, and sank down behind a shelter. For a moment or two he heard nothing and his hopes rose — then he heard a crash-splash from the stream, the pad of running feet, and they burst into the half-circle of huts. They took a pace or two then stopped. Jason held his breath. Slowly, ever so slowly, the feet shifted round and then they stopped again, pointing at his lean-to, and he heard the spring-click of an automatic being cocked.

Jason let out his breath in a deep sigh. He pushed himself up to a half-crouch and stared over the leafy framework, and his eyes met those of his pursuer.

The Japanese took a short pace forward and swung up the muzzle of his gun. In the sudden silence the chug of the diesel sounded closer, drifting to them clearly, and the hijacker hesitated, then let the weapon swing down to his side. Eyes still holding Jason's he flexed his arms and with forearm, wrist and hand held edgewise ready to chop, advanced on the boy.

Jason backed away — then his eye fell on the blowpipe, propped against the little shelter, and he snatched it up and stood waiting, holding the long tube like a pike. The Japanese smiled in contempt as he reached out to pluck aside the flimsy leaf framework, when Jason with a shock remembered the dart. He sprang back, swung up the blowpipe, set the mouthpiece to his lips and blew fiercely and with all his might.

The hijacker's hand seized the lean-to and gripped it, but his eyes looked down to the pith head of a dart, sprouting from his open shirt front. He looked up again

64

and began to pull round his weapon, but Jason swung back his arm and threw the blowpipe like a javelin, and it struck the hijacker in the forehead with a heavy thud. His head went back and Jason turned, ran a few yards down the path then ducked away among the trees. From the direction of the huts he heard a crashing sound, as if the lean-to was being dragged down, and a hoarse, gasping cry, but he only ran the faster. When at last he stopped, thoroughly winded, from behind him there was only silence.

5
BUILD-UP

Jason moved across to a tree, leant his shoulder against it and let his head fall against the smooth bark, and stood there, gasping for breath and trying to listen, but he heard only the blood pounding in his ears and the thud-thud, thud-thud of his pumping heart. Then he heard, or thought he heard, something rustle back the way he had come and so he set off away from the spur as fast as he could run – but the broken ground, littered with fallen, rotted trunks, the tangling undergrowth and his growing exhaustion all began to tell. He slowed to a trot and then to a weary stumble. He pushed his way forward more and more slowly, and at last came to a full stop, head hanging and chest and lungs bursting.

For long minutes he stayed there, while the sweat cooled and dried on him, while feeling and strength crept back into his legs and thighs, and hope into his mind. There seemed to be nothing moving near him: he had got clear away from that hijacker – that dart must have affected him, probably made him too sick to follow immediately, or possibly the blow on the head had knocked him out. Also, he now had a good idea of where he himself was; he had not run on *beyond* the spur, but *back,* and therefore back towards the aircraft – and the slight downhill slope below him could only lead to the sea. There was something else, something nagging at his mind, and he remembered: just as the hijacker had spotted him they had both heard the sound of the marine diesel. At last there might be help for the injured and some relief for the sweltering hostages, for those children! Impatiently he began to make his way down the slope towards the sea.

In less than a quarter of an hour he caught the glint of sunshine through the leaves ahead. He slowed down, cautious once more. There were the same thickets at the edge of the trees and the same wall of pale green, rhododendron-like leaves, and he crawled in below the rubbery stems till he could peer out. The beach was empty. He wrinkled his eyes against the sun's glare and peered out to sea, and saw with a slight shock of disappointment that the sea too was empty. The fishing boat had gone, and there was no sign of other craft.

Then, as Jason lay there, gazing out at the open beach and the empty sea, he heard a sudden harsh racketing from the ridge behind; it roared above his head and dwindled over beyond the promontory, where the airliner lay beached. He crashed out through the wall of leaves, ran through the line of palms and from the open beach caught a quick glimpse of the helicopter as it swung and dipped. Prudently he dodged back in among the palms and, looking sharply about him, running, walking a few steps then breaking into a run again, hurried back to the beach he had left not quite fourteen hours ago.

The first Thai soldier stood where the palms ended and the open lallang began. Rifle slung and humming to himself he was gazing with interest down at the beached airliner, and at his officer unsuccessfully trying to communicate with a Japanese who had him covered with a sub-machine-gun. The rest of the Thai section were spread out at intervals well back from the aircraft, also staring at it and at the faces which jammed the open passenger door and the window glass. At first the soldier paid no heed to the low whistle from the fringe of bushes behind him: there was considerable background noise; the racket of the first helicopter was dying away and a second was approaching. Jason whistled again, without success, then tried a shout: 'Hey, there – hullo!'

The soldier looked round and in an instant had his rifle up and was staring over the sights at the apparition peering at him through the leaves – a pale face beneath tangled brown hair and a naked chest and shoulders scored with long deep scratches.

Quickly Jason put his finger to his lips and indicated the aircraft with a warning gesture. Still the soldier gaped at him, again Jason put his finger to his lips and the soldier backed away a yard or two and began calling out to the man nearest him, some forty yards away. Jason groaned: this idiot would soon have hijackers and everyone else staring up towards them – when the racket of rotor blades roared up over the tree-tops and the second helicopter settled on the nearest corner of the grassy strip. Half a dozen soldiers tumbled out and scurried below the whirling blades towards the palms while three others hastily unloaded canvas containers and began dragging them towards the trees. As soon as they were clear, the helicopter took off and swung away low over the sea, and another settled in its place. But after the first eruption of soldiers a more sedate figure clambered down – a short bulky man in a light suit, who hardly bothered to duck his head for the rotor blades as he walked briskly towards the beach.

A great deal then began to happen at once. The young officer appeared; the soldier, still pointing his rifle at Jason, called out and the officer looked in astonishment – then caught sight of the civilian and clapped a hand to his helmet in a salute of furious intensity. With a lift of the finger which had the officer running to him, still saluting, he walked to where Jason crouched behind the leaves, and after looking him up and down said in clipped, careful English, 'Good afternoon.'

'Good afternoon,' replied Jason mechanically, still crouching.

Brown eyes, expressionless in the smooth, heavy face, studied him. 'You have come from the plane.'

'Yes. I escaped last night.' Then Jason burst out: 'You must help them! There are four men wounded. I think one is dying. There was a fight.' Words tumbled out of him, everything he'd been thinking about since he heard the helicopters: 'It's hot, it's very hot in there, and there are children – '

'Wait here.' The bulky man set off swiftly down towards the plane and desperately Jason called after him: 'Don't tell them I'm here! They don't know where I am!' The man lifted a hand without looking round and the young officer ran to catch him up. Jason watched them anxiously from the screen of leaves. Up came the sub-machine-gun muzzle as the two approached, but to Jason's surprise the foremost gun muzzle lowered again. The hijackers actually seemed to be talking, though one of them kept the officer in his sights. A third ran back to beneath the nose of the airliner and Jason caught a glimpse of someone moving in the pilot's cabin, then the hijacker turned back and spoke to the civilian. He replied, turned and walked back up to where Jason crouched, hidden. 'We will move round out of sight,' he said, and followed by an orderly and the young officer, he moved off through the belt of palms. Jason kept parallel with them behind the fringe of bushes till they were out of direct sight of the aircraft and then pushed out through the bushes to meet them.

'I am Colonel Chula, of the Interior Ministry,' said the bulky man. He smiled wryly. 'That is why they salute me so efficiently. What is your name?'

'Jason Wright.'

'When our station medical officer arrives the Japanese will allow him on board.' Colonel Chula looked Jason up and down. 'But you need medical attention yourself – and some clothing.' He said a word to the platoon commander, who clapped a hand to his helmet brim and, still saluting, repeated the order and doubled off to where the signallers were busy stringing up an aerial. In a moment the medical orderly arrived, saluted and swung round his first-aid haversack.

'Sit down,' said Colonel Chula, 'he will treat your cuts.'

'I'd rather he did my feet first.' Jason sat and turned up one foot.

'Ai-yah!' exclaimed the orderly at the mass of embedded thorn spines. Colonel Chula narrowed his eyes. 'You were walking in the forest.'

Suddenly cautious, Jason said: 'Not very far; I found a thorn bush.'

The medical orderly sponged Jason's chest and shoulders with an antiseptic solution, then spent some time plucking at the spines in his feet with a pair of tweezers, but most of them resisted his efforts. Eventually he stopped, shaking his head and speaking in Thai to the Colonel.

'He says that you will have to have these taken out by a doctor. He does not have the equipment. We have a small field hospital arriving by air later today.' Colonel Chula smiled faintly. 'You will be their first patient.'

A third helicopter settled, the lallang flattened in the down-blast of the rotors and dust flew, from it ran more men in uniform and the Colonel exclaimed in satisfaction: 'Here is our medical officer.'

A young man in olive-green uniform and slung about with bulging medical haversacks hurried towards him, they had a quick conversation, he nodded, gave a sketchy salute and ran towards the aircraft. 'They will let him on,' said Colonel Chula. 'It is arranged. Now the wounded will be seen to.'

Jason licked his parched lips. The sun was hot, outside the forest. Even in the patchy shade of the palms he felt the strength of it, and the growing heat seemed to lie on his skin like a blanket. More and more dust was being blown up by the helicopters, and he felt the touch of grit on his tongue and between his teeth. 'Have you any water?'

'Better than water.' Colonel Chula lifted a hand, and two soldiers busy tying out an awning nearby dropped it and ran up. *'Mapraw,'* he said. They looked at Jason, and smiled with gleams of white teeth. One stripped off his webbing equipment and helmet and the other handed him a short length of rope from a kitbag. He chose a palm,

71

passed the rope loosely round the trunk and himself, and knotted it. He jerked back against it once or twice and, satisfied, jumped up to grip the trunk with his insteps, pushed up, lifted the rope, pushed up again ... Up and up he went while Jason gaped: he had seldom seen anything so smooth and apparently effortless. In a few moments the Thai soldier was perched high above him among the feathery fronds and twisting at the first green coconut. He called down a warning and with a whiz of air a heavy coconut thudded to the ground. The second man drew a broad knife from his belt and with a series of skilful chops cut through the thick pith, then, using the heavy blade with the delicacy of a penknife, he cut a circular hole in the soft inner shell and offered it to Jason: *'Karuna!'*

Obediently Jason took the coconut with both hands, put back his head and let the liquid run into his mouth. It tasted rather of lemon, and he swallowed greedily, but what surprised him most was its coldness. There was so much that he was quite unable to finish it, and it was still half-full when he put it down on the sand. For the moment he felt better, and as he heard the racket of a helicopter taking off, he asked: 'Where are they from?'

'Hat Yai airfield.' Colonel Chula waved a hand towards the west. 'Not many miles.'

'How did you find out about us?'

'A fishing boat saw the plane early this morning. I was visiting the Hat Yai air base, and as soon as we heard by telephone we flew in this first platoon, and more men and supplies are being flown down from Bangkok. It is awkward, for we are busy elsewhere.' He looked round as a soldier came up, hand at the salute, and indicated the awning tied out among the palms.

'Some shelter is ready.' Colonel Chula looked at Jason.

'Come. We will sit down and soon you will have some food.'

The shelter, equipped with a folding canvas chair and half a dozen equipment containers, did little more than give shade, but to Jason it looked like a palace – and he thought with a pang of the people stifling in the plane. 'Will the hijackers get what they want? When will we know?'

'That is difficult to say – our Government will do all it can. But before everything we must send news to your parents; they will be happy to hear that you are safe.' He gestured and a signaller appeared with pencil and message pad. 'Please write down your father's name and address. Our signaller will transmit this for your Embassy in Bangkok. They will inform him by telephone.'

'No! They must not be told!'

Colonel Chula raised his eyebrows at Jason's outburst.

'They must not be told,' repeated Jason in agitation. 'The newspapers will get it and the radio news, and the hijackers will hear it when they listen on their set! They will know I am here!'

'But why should they not know that you are safe?'

'They may demand my return.'

For a moment Colonel Chula studied Jason, then said slowly: 'That is quite possible. However, I can arrange that your father is told secretly and asked to remain silent. Will that do?'

'Yes, that will be all right.' Jason felt a twinge of guilt at having tried to protect himself at the price of his parents' frantic worry, and then felt that he had another reason for not wanting the hijackers to know that he was safe with the authorities – though what this was he could not make out.

'I think that you are right to keep your presence a secret from them,' said Colonel Chula. He took a small case from his pocket, extracted and lit a dark cheroot and sat smoking reflectively. 'I was able to talk a little to these men. During the war, when Thailand was occupied for four years by the Japanese Army, all officer cadets had to study their language. It was not very popular, and I quickly forgot most of it, but I can remember a little. That is why they spoke to me.'

Jason remembered his surprise at seeing the stony-faced hijackers apparently unbend and speak.

'After I had arranged about the medical officer, they said something I could not understand properly – something about one man being missing. They were very threatening. They must mean you, Mister Jason.'

Jason said nothing. The hijackers had *not* meant him; they had meant the man who had followed him into the forest. He could not have returned, and that meant – his heart sank – that the man was dead. He clenched his teeth to stop his jaw trembling. Was it murder? Surely it was self-defence! But if those Japanese found out, if they ever got hold of him . . . He felt rather sick.

'I think that you need rest,' Colonel Chula looked searchingly at Jason. 'You look very tired. But first, can you tell me all you remember about the Japanese?'

'Yes.' Jason tried to get some order into his thoughts. He kept seeing visions of the hijacker reaching out for him, looking down at the dart sprouting from his ribs, his head going back with the thud of the blowpipe butt; then the sounds, the crash of leaves and the strangled cry –

He had tried to persuade himself that they hadn't really happened, and he'd been nearly successful, until now. 'Yes,' Jason repeated. He must talk sense, tell him all he saw; but what if Colonel Chula, this man with the impassive face and searching eyes, what if he found out? But he was waiting.

Jason took a deep breath and cleared his throat. 'There

were – there are five,' he said, correcting himself quickly, 'three men and two women.'

'Two *women?*' For the first time Jason saw Colonel Chula look really surprised.

'Well, one man dressed as a woman, maybe two – ' He stopped. He was explaining it all very badly. His jaw muscles felt heavy, clumsy with fear. That Jap was dead, the others were not many yards away and they were going to make trouble. He was trembling.

Colonel Chula spoke, but in Thai, Jason caught the whiff of spirits and the orderly handed him a small, heavy glass with an inch of orange-coloured liquid in it, and added water.

'That will steady you for now, and afterwards you can sleep.' The Colonel's expression was one of concern, and Jason tried to pull himself together. Unless he made a better job of explaining, he might as well have stayed in the aircraft. He nodded, lifted the glass, sniffed at it, then started to drink it as if it were lemonade. He choked and Colonel Chula said, 'Head back, toss it down,' and Jason did so.

He blinked at the warm, resinous taste of it. Nothing much seemed to be happening. He took a breath and began again – and found that suddenly he was talking confidently. 'We didn't pay them any attention until the pilot anounced the hijack,' he said. 'Then three of them – one certainly wearing women's clothes – settled in the back, aft. I heard one passenger say something about a bomb . . .'

Everything he said was noted down, sketches of the aircraft layout made, and the positions of the explosives fixed under the fuel tanks marked. Colonel Chula then went over the notes with Jason, and only when he was satisfied did he at last sit back and say: 'For you, food and sleep.' His orderly led Jason back a hundred yards out of sight beyond the promontory, where a groundsheet had been tied out, with two folded blankets beneath it.

The temporary stimulation of the brandy and water had left him, and Jason's mind was heavy with foreboding. He refused the plate of cold food the orderly offered him. When he had awakened this morning, he could have eaten a horse, but now his stomach seemed to have contracted; he could not have swallowed a single mouthful. He began to curse himself for his rashness in escaping. He should have stayed and done the less romantic task of looking after those two children. He had abandoned them, and now he was going to pay for it. Miserable, he lay back on the rough blanket, staring up at the groundsheet above him, the sun's rays overhead shining through. It was still barely mid-day, but he had been furiously active since first light, only once stopping for rest, when he had collapsed with exhaustion and fright. The oppressive heat, the strain of the long morning and now this new, double-edged threat exhausted him. What on earth could he do? Ignoring the noisy background of another helicopter-load arriving and the more distant, heavier beat of a marine diesel from the sea, he lay endlessly turning over and over in his mind the dilemma he was in, till at last, like a fuse melting through, the taut wire of his worries parted and he fell into a heavy sleep.

'Tan!'

Jason opened his eyes, blinked at the smiling Thai orderly with the cup of tea, and remembered. 'Thanks.' The tea, without milk or sugar, was bitter but refreshing, and he sipped at it slowly while he looked round and got his bearings. He stood up, yawning. Then he saw neatly stacked on a folded towel beside him a soldier's jungle-green uniform, and he put it on. Although long enough, the shirt and trousers – made for slim Thais – were a trifle tight, but the green canvas shoes fitted well enough, as did the canvas hat.

The long shadows of the palms stretched down the beach towards the sea. He looked at his watch and saw with surprise that it was nearly five o'clock; he had been asleep for nearly four hours. He felt enormously better, and in perspective his worries and fears seemed less immediate. All he had to do was to keep a grip on himself and keep his mouth shut.

Beyond the promontory he saw threads of smoke rising from among the palms, and from the ridge behind again came the familiar racket of a helicopter. He walked along the line of palms, reached the corner above the promontory, slipped round it – and stood staring.

The shore was swarming with men, except for a broad space round the aircraft itself, cordoned off with ropes and stakes at which stood Thai sentries. Jason could see at least two of the hijackers under the wings, but below the tail section he could see figures in the shallows of the incoming tide. He made out women's dresses, and was sure he saw two small figures with them. He sighed with relief: the hijackers – probably more confident now that sentries had been put round them – had at least allowed the women and children down. Tents were being pitched among the palms and in front of these three small marquees were already up, one with a Red Cross flag hanging from a guy-rope. Taking care to keep well out of sight of the shore, Jason walked through the working parties and looked from behind a marquee. A coastal fishing boat lay at anchor further round from Speedwing II, being unloaded by soldiers in water to their waists, and half-way along the beach, some hundreds of yards beyond the scarred and flattened gap in the lallang, more tents were being pitched. They were set conspicuously apart, and Jason guessed that they might be for the soldiers.

At an unfamiliar engine note he looked towards the grassy strip. A light aircraft was touching down, and from it clambered two Europeans, slung about with cameras and tape recorders and carrying zip bags. They were at once intercepted by a military policeman in a white-painted helmet, who pointed to the distant tent village. The two men expostulated but Jason saw the Thai shake his head and again point to the tent village.

'Journalists!' Colonel Chula had come silently from the marquee. 'Soon they will be here by the dozen. We have prepared a reception area for them.' His heavy face was suddenly grim. 'I am going to see that they do not get in our way. Now,' he said, his tone relaxed once more, 'I am expecting someone who will want to ask you some more questions, but while we are waiting go to the hospital tent. The doctor there will see to your feet.'

Inside, he found it equipped with stretcher beds, folding chairs, chests of stainless steel instruments and electric lamps with cable leading out to a portable generator. A Thai doctor and two nursing orderlies were busy laying out their equipment, but as Jason came in, the doctor straightened up and gave him a beaming smile. 'Mister Jason Wright! Colonel Chula said you'd be coming along!' He exuded an air of professional competence and Jason was intrigued to hear him speak with a pronounced American accent; rimless glasses heightened the trans-atlantic impression. 'Will you please sit down, Jason, and remove your shoes? Ah, yes!' The doctor studied the soles of his feet carefully. 'I think we can deal with those for you! Now if you would just lie down!' He indicated the examination couch, and Jason stretched out on it. 'Yes, I think perhaps a small local anaesthetic –' He talked busily as he worked, but studiously made no reference to the hijacking or to Jason's escape. One thing puzzled Jason, however, and in a break in the flow of talk he asked:

'Where are the injured men from the plane – have they been sent out?'

'No, Jason, they have not.' The doctor spoke in a deliberately conversational tone. 'The Japanese hijackers allowed our young medical officer on board, and have since allowed on supplies of all kinds, but they have not allowed the injured men to go – nor have they let the medical officer go, either. It seems,' he said, working carefully at Jason's feet, 'that anyone who goes on board becomes their prisoner.'

'But the injured men – '

'I know; it seems barbaric to hold them. I guess,' he added, 'that the Japanese may have some other reason for holding them. Now,' he said briskly, standing up and showing Jason a lint pad liberally covered with dark thorn-points, some half an inch long. 'You should walk more easily now! We'll just put on a light dressing.'

'Thank you very much indeed, Doctor.' Jason swung his feet round and pulled his shoes on carefully over the dressings. He stood up, feeling curiously clumsy, and the doctor smiled: 'The anaesthetic has not yet worn off – your feet are still numb. By the way, please see your own doctor in England on your return. I expect you'll be there in forty-eight hours!'

'I expect so, Doctor,' replied Jason politely, but for a moment he was taken aback: the thought of simply flying off to England had not occurred to him. He thanked the doctor again, shook hands and went outside – just in time to see Colonel Chula hurrying off towards the corner of the strip where a helicopter was settling and men in uniform disgorging from it.

Not all the new arrivals were Thai soldiers; two wore plain clothes, and as Jason watched Colonel Chula greet them he felt a quick ripple of alarm. Although two hundred yards away, there was no mistaking the stocky, powerful figures, the stiff, formal bows as they shook hands and the pause before they straightened up, erect once more. The two men were Japanese.

Jason watched uneasily as the little group walked up the soft sand towards the marquee and stopped deep in talk outside it. Then Colonel Chula caught sight of Jason and said something to the two men. They both turned, he stood uncomfortably under their unblinking gaze, then they vanished into the marquee. Some minutes later the orderly called Jason inside. The two men rose from camp chairs and Colonel Chula got up from the folding table.

'Mr Matsutan and Mr Sumitomo have been sent by the Japanese Government to help. They are from the Tokyo Special Branch.'

'Matsutan.' The elder of the two, a middle-aged man with cropped, grizzled hair, gave Jason a deep bow.

'Sumitomo.' The second man was much younger, in his early twenties, and wore his black hair long, brushed back over his ears. He bowed rather less stiffly and Jason shook hands with them both.

'We heard that you had escaped and brought the news.' Matsutan bowed again, and Jason noted that his English, though clipped, was good.

'No.' At Matsutan's look of surprise Jason said quickly: 'I did escape, but a fishing boat saw the aircraft first.'

'That is correct,' confirmed Colonel Chula. 'Mister Jason came from the forest. I found him just at the back of the palms here.'

'Ah so.' Matsutan thought a moment. 'You did not reach a village?'

'No.'

'Did you go along the beach in the morning?'

'No, I thought it was too open. I walked in the forest till I heard a helicopter, and came back.'

Then Matsutan asked the question that Jason had dreaded. 'Did anyone follow you?'

'I think one man tried to swim after me, but I got away in the darkness.' Jason shot a quick glance at Colonel Chula but he, eyes half-shut over his cheroot, made no comment.

Matsutan murmured something in Japanese, stood and bowed first to Jason and then to Colonel Chula. 'Perhaps now we will go to the aircraft?'

When the two Japanese had set off Jason rose to go but as he left, the Colonel called after him: 'We expect some British gentlemen soon, from Bangkok. They are waiting their turn for a helicopter at Hat Yai. Soon you will be able to leave.'

Feeling more uneasy than ever, Jason wandered aimlessly about, watching the Thai soldiers busy roping off their tented enclosure and the headquarters' marquees, and erecting a big sign in front of it: 'OFF LIMITS'. When Colonel Chula said he wasn't going to have journalists getting in the way, clearly he meant it. Gazing across at their tents – still being erected – Jason saw with considerable surprise that Thai villagers had arrived, apparently from nowhere, and were busy setting up little stalls, probably to sell fruit and vegetables. He had seen no one walk along this beach from the north, so presumably their village must lie to the south. He sighed; he had set out to walk the wrong way.

He paid little attention when yet another helicopter landed in its private duststorm, but jerked round at the sound of an English voice: 'Hullo there!' A tall man in check shirt, slacks and faded desert boots was striding towards him, hand outstretched. 'Michael Deane, from the Embassy. You must be Jason Wright. We got through to Hong Kong on the scrambler, and our people there have told your parents – all strictly secret!' He clapped

Jason on the shoulder. 'Wonderful piece of work! As soon as you've given us the story and the Thais release you, we'll get you out of this. You may have to spend the night at Hat Yai, but you'll be in Bangkok tomorrow morning.'

Jason felt a warm rush of relief. Soon he'd be away from this ominous beach, away from Colonel Chula with his impassive face and watchful eyes and away from that Japanese – what was his name, Matsu something? – and his awkward questions. Also, once and for all, he would be away from those murdering hijackers.

By the helicopter pad two other Englishmen were heaving at suitcases and a large crate of equipment, and Jason and the tall man ran down to help them drag it out of reach of the helicopter rotors. As soon as they had man-handled the baggage up to the tents, Deane introduced them. 'This is Charles Edwards, from the airline, and Bill Williams, from the Foreign Office communications branch.'

'Hi, there,' said Williams. He winked. 'You're better off here than there!' and he jerked his head towards the plane. Unaccountably Jason felt his euphoria recede.

'Nasty business, this,' said Edwards. He spoke very seriously. 'They're a desperate bunch, and I don't like the look of things at all.' He looked sombrely at Jason. 'You did well to get away. How did you manage it – through the emergency hatch?'

'Not the one by the starboard wing,' said Jason, and Edwards looked surprised. 'I found a panel in one of the washrooms,' Jason explained. 'It had a sort of catch and I opened it.' He paused a moment at the deepening dismay in the other's face. 'There was a compartment with a lot of pipes in it –'

'The hydraulic bay.' Edwards looked closely at Jason. 'Are your eyes painful? Have you had any trouble seeing since you got out?'

'No, what's wrong?'

'That hydraulic fluid blinds. I'm surprised there wasn't some about, the pipes must have been strained during that landing. You've had no pain?'

'No. I shut my eyes when I was climbing over, against the fumes.'

'Did you rub them at all?'

'No time – I was straight down into the water. It probably washed my eyes out.'

'You were lucky – one touch of that stuff and you'd have been blinded, and screaming your head off as well. Never try that again, d'you hear me?'

Jason nodded, silent. He was beginning to find out that things could be more complicated than they at first seemed.

'Well,' said Michael Deane, 'at least you're out safely. Now I'll explain what's going on. I'm here to represent British interests but, as you will understand, the Thai Government is handling all this, and they're doing it very efficiently, too. Things are humming in Bangkok, and they're very busy indeed internationally over these hijackers' demands. Your information was of great help. But,' he added, looking at Jason very intently, 'before you leave, I'd like you to rack your brains. Is there anything you may have missed? It's always possible that there is something that you have since remembered, that will help us get those passengers freed. If you think that there is anything – anything at all – tell me. It might be terribly important.'

Jason was silent. The mere fact that the hijackers had sent a man to kill him didn't really signify anything; it was probably their fury at his escape, and yes, that must be it! – he would be an example to the others, a warning not to try. Why hadn't he thought of it before? Again he felt that warm rush of relief. 'No,' he said, smiling, 'I don't think there's a single thing.'

'Good!' Deane clapped him on the shoulder once more. 'I'll go and ask if we can get you out of here on the next lift.' He turned aside to have a word with Edwards, and Bill Williams called across to Jason, 'You look cheery! Glad to be off, eh?' He gestured towards the beach with a screwdriver. 'I'll bet there's a few down there'd give a quid or two to swop places with you!' He looked up into the sky. 'Here's a helicopter. You'll probably be off in ten minutes!'

For the second time Jason felt that warm, cosy feeling of relief recede, but this time it drained away altogether, leaving him with a cold feeling of having been guilty of betrayal. Those two children, the three men who'd had a go, Sue and the other stewardesses, Captain Chisholm, the big Chinese who'd sat next to him – all were down there three or four hundred yards away, waiting while others decided whether they lived or were burnt to death. He, Jason, had tried to do something for them all – but in the event it had not been necessary, and although no one else knew it, he might well have made things worse. More dust whirled up as the helicopter settled.

'Jason!' Michael Deane came running back from the direction of the beach. 'I've just had a word with Colonel Chula down at the aircraft. He's pretty busy down there, but he releases you, and sends his regards. Come along, we might just get you on that helicopter.'

Jason hesitated, but for no more than a moment. 'I'm not going.'

'Hurry up, or you'll miss it.' Deane did not seem to have heard, and Jason said more loudly: 'You don't understand. I don't want to go, I'll stay – maybe I can help.'

Deane turned an astonished face towards him. 'You've passed on everything you know, you can't do more than that!' He took Jason's elbow. 'Hurry, man – you're wasting time!'

Jason pulled away. 'I don't want to go.' He began to feel that he was behaving like a fool, but he said doggedly, 'I may be able to do something. I just can't go while the others are still down there.'

Michael Deane opened his mouth to speak again, saw the desperate face, paused and then said mildly, 'Very well. But you were expected in Bangkok.'

'I'm sorry; I don't want to cause anyone any trouble.'

'All right, then – and I know how you feel. But perhaps I should tell you that your father is on his way to Bangkok to see you. It was to have been a surprise.'

Jason was silent for a moment, then muttered, 'I won't go. He'll understand.'

'Yes, I expect he will. Now, if you're staying, we'll get you fixed up in our tent. If you want to do something useful, give Bill a hand with his set. I've one or two things to discuss with the Thais.'

'You changed your mind pretty smartly! Anything rather than school, eh?' Williams handed Jason a pair of pliers. 'I want you to draw out these pins from this case. Carefully, now – there's an expensive set in here.' He went on chatting, keeping Jason busy till gradually he felt the turmoil within him subside. That feeling of spurious warmth, he recognized, had been the relief of surrender, no more; now, though still desperately worried, he no longer felt that sense of guilt.

'That's it!' Williams straightened up. 'Before we do any more I'll have to check up on an aerial siting. I don't want it to clash with these others.' He moved off to speak to the Thai signallers and Jason stood idly waiting. Voices came to him through the marquee canvas, voices he recognized. There was Colonel Chula, then he heard Michael Deane's clear English voice, and the curt voice of Matsutan. They must have finished at the aircraft. Jason pricked up his ears. Matsutan was explaining something,

something ominous. 'These men say they have one man missing.'

'That's the boy, of course.'

'No, it is one of their own men. They sent him along the beach this morning to look for the boy, and he did not return.'

'Perhaps he ran away!'

'He would not run away.' Matsutan's voice was hard and convincing. 'I know these people.'

'What do they expect us to do about it?'

'They think we have captured him and have taken him away in a helicopter.'

'But that's preposterous! Did you say we knew nothing about it?'

'I did say that. They do not believe me.'

'Colonel Chula, you haven't got this man, have you?'

'No, and I have told them. They did not believe me either.'

'Well,' said Deane, 'there isn't much we can do about it, is there? This chap may be anywhere!'

'We must do something about it,' said Matsutan in his curt voice, while outside the marquee wall Jason listened appalled. 'They say that unless we return this man in twenty-four hours they are going to execute two steward-esses – one English, one Chinese.'

6

MATSUTAN

INSIDE the marquee the tense discussion went on, but Jason wandered away between the tents. His worst fears were being realized, as subconsciously he had known all along they would be. The hijackers were not going meekly to accept the disappearance of one of their number – and when they found out that he was not merely a prisoner, but dead, killed by one of their own hostages, their fury would be terrible. Jason crouched by the bole of a palm, staring out at the darkening sea. He did not know how long he had been sitting there when he heard his name called, and he got up and walked slowly back. Swift evening was coming, and Thai soldiers were lighting and distributing hurricane lamps.

'Supper, Jason!' Deane called to him. 'Come on, it's cold, but it'll hold us till breakfast!' The three were busy opening a giant woven-cane basket and taking out plastic cups and plates, cold chicken, bottles of cordial, a huge thermos of soup – the hamper seemed bottomless. 'Ambassador's special, this thing – specially designed for Embassy picnics!' Deane spoke cheerfully. 'If it weren't for these miserable hijackers, this'd be great fun!'

Jason forced a smile. He hadn't eaten much since that ham steak for yesterday's breakfast, but still he couldn't have faced a mouthful of food. Before hearing Matsutan's chilling announcement he'd begun to feel almost normal and had been looking forward to a meal, but now he felt as if a stone lay cold and hard in his stomach.

'Jason, some chicken,' Bill passed him across a plate and began piling slices of breast and a chicken leg on it, but the sight of the food made Jason feel slightly sick, and he passed the plate back. 'Nothing for me, thanks – it's still a bit warm. I think I'll just go for a walk along this beach at the back.'

Deane shot the others a swift glance, then replied briskly: 'Of course. But keep a watch out – these journalists are beginning to stream in, and we can't order *them* to keep quiet about you.'

'All right.' Jason left the lamp-lit line of tents behind and walked slowly along beside the palms, listening to the sea hiss on the sand. On his left the forest ridge was black against the night sky, and he stopped and gazed up at it. Somewhere in there the missing hijacker lay dead, and tomorrow his companions would carry out their savage threat when he did not return. Jason crossed the beach and wandered along the high-water mark. The tide was coming in, and he thought back to his escape the night before. Then he had been full of confidence – arrogance, almost – like those hijackers, certain of the rightness of his action and vaguely aware of the glory his exploit might bring. And now? He stopped once more and stood staring out seawards into the darkness striving to find a way out, some escape, anything – but always he came back to the bitter fact that, unless he spoke, two innocents would die.

He stood there till the tide crept to his feet. It receded but came up again, this time soaking his shoes, and, at the chill touch of the sea-water, Jason woke as if from a dream. Nothing would wait. He must choose, but he had known from the beginning what his choice must be. Heavily he turned back to confess.

From the line of camp fires glowing sparks floated up and died high among the palm fronds, and the tinkle of an orchestra of gongs and flutes drifted from a soldier's transistor, but in the main marquee Thai signallers were busy as Colonel Chula sat working with his staff. Jason glanced in past the sentry, but seeing the numbers inside he hesitated. Perhaps he'd tell Colonel Chula a little later, when he was less busy. Going to tell Michael Deane was the easiest and the most obvious thing to do – but, Jason admitted, it was also the most cowardly. He'd tell Colonel Chula straight. After all, it was Colonel Chula he'd lied to; he might as well tell him the truth himself. He'd wait a short while till he could get him alone.

He moved out beyond the marquee, safe in the darkness. The sky paled and he watched as the moon rose over the eastern sea, a moon just past the full. In daylight a beached whale, in moonlight, with the tide up around it, Speedwing II looked a swan on the water, and for a moment Jason stood lost in contemplation. Near him sand crunched. It was the Japanese detective, Matsutan, with Sumitomo beside him. Together they stood silent, gazing out at the moon's path on the dark sea.

' "*Omo-koto,*
    Nado to hito no,
    Nakaruran?" ' murmured Matsutan, and Sumitomo replied:

' "*Aogeba sora ni,*
    Tsuki no sayakeki." '

Jason glanced at the shadowy figure and Matsutan translated:

' "Why lost in thought – has no one asked?" and the reply is:

"Lifting my eyes, I see the moon in its glory." The monk Ji-en composed that *tanka* eight hundred years ago.'

No one spoke for a moment. 'But there is more than the moon to think on,' Matsutan continued. 'When I stand here on the shore, I think on all those in their prison so close in front of us. You, too, Jason – you were thinking of your friends when you escaped.'

Jason nodded. The moon was rising quickly and by its light he saw Matsutan's sombre expression as he gazed down at the aircraft, roped off in its enclosure. The hiss of the sea was closer.

'You must have thought of your friends when you were in the forest,' said Matsutan.

'Yes.'

'You were long in the forest, Jason.'

Jason sighed. The burden of his secret was becoming too much to bear, and Matsutan, with the silent Sumitomo, was asking to share it. 'Yes,' he said, 'I was long in the forest. I was hiding from one man.'

'The man who followed you in the sea?'

'I don't know. I saw him on the beach the next morning. He ran after me into the forest.' He hesitated, and went on: 'I hid, but he found me again.'

Matsutan and Sumitomo stood motionless, as if by moving they might break the spell of the moonlight and startle Jason into silence.

'I found some – ' he hesitated over the word ' – aborigines. They ran away, leaving a blowpipe.' He made a tube of his two curled hands and blew through it. 'When the hijacker came, I shot a dart into him,' indicating his stomach, 'then struck him here,' and he touched his forehead. 'I think he is dead.' He waited a moment, still no one spoke, and he said wearily: 'I am sorry I did not tell you this before.' Jason was glad of the concealing dark. Somehow it made confession easier. 'I will go and tell Colonel Chula.'

'No. Wait.'

He paused in surprise. 'But he will want to know quickly,' he said, feeling rather sick again. 'We must tell the hijackers.'

'Are you sure this man is dead? Did you see him?'

'No.'

'Perhaps he is not dead, but only wounded.'

It was a straw, and Jason clutched at it. 'Maybe! Yes, maybe he is hurt – or lost!'

There was a rapid mutter in Japanese, then Matsutan said: 'I think it would be best if we go quickly to see this place.'

'Now? With a torch?'

Jason saw a brief gleam of teeth. 'Not now,' said Matsutan. 'It is not possible to move under the trees in the darkness. But we will go early in the morning. Where will you sleep?'

'In the tent with Mr Deane and the others.'

'Please arrange to sleep outside your tent. We will come for you before dawn. It would be better for no one else to know.' There was a pause; the two Japanese bowed stiffly, and Jason gave an awkward duck of the head in reply. They did not move and he saw that they were waiting for him to go, so walked away, bypassing the main marquee and coming round to the tents behind.

'Hullo, Jason – there you are!' Michael Deane waved at him from outside the tent door. 'Cup of coffee?' The three were eating biscuits and drinking from enamel mugs, and Bill poured out a mug for Jason from a saucepan propped beside a round, fire-scorched tin. He saw Jason's glance and explained: 'Desert cooking – tin, bit of sand, dash of petrol – very quick, if you're careful! I'll show you tomorrow. Biscuit? Go on – try one, you've eaten nothing!'

To please him Jason took a biscuit and bit at it, but he ate without relish. The coffee, though – that helped. It was scalding, and he sipped gratefully at the strong, sugary brew. The others were talking diplomatic technicalities, and to his surprise Jason found himself yawning widely. He had thought that after his heavy sleep that afternoon he would remain wakeful, but he felt his eyelids drooping. He blinked and looked up to see Deane watching him. 'Tired?'

Jason nodded. 'Yes, pretty tired.'

'Bill here's going to be busy tonight; he's got a pretty full programme of listening, but he shouldn't disturb you. If you'd like to kip down straight away, I suggest you get down to it in that corner, away from the light. Can we fix you up with blankets?'

'I've got some, thanks. I think I'll sleep out under the fly-sheet, it's a bit cooler.'

'Just as you like. Sleep well, then.'

Earlier the Thai orderly had brought him the two blankets he had used that afternoon, and Jason laid one out under the flysheet, took off his shoes and rolled himself in the other. He thought for a moment of mosquitoes, then how cool it was with the night breeze from the sea.

'Jason.' A torch flashed briefly and went out. 'It will soon be dawn.'

He sat up. The flysheet above him was soaked with dew and the sand was damp and cold. Its touch took him back to the morning before, and at once he was fully awake. Shivering he groped about for his canvas shoes, found them, and pulled them on with a care for his damp dressings. 'Ready,' he whispered. 'Shall I lead?'

'Please!'

The tide was coming in again, but this time the foam of the waves was shot through with points of green fire. Seeing the phosphorescence the Japanese murmured to each other, and Sumitomo explained in a low voice: 'Maybe storm at sea.'

Jason led along the beach confidently enough, but after

three hundred yards slowed down. He had hoped to find his and the hijacker's footprints leading up towards the palms and the forest, but it was not yet light enough to see well, and in a whisper he explained.

Matsutan looked back towards the tents. 'We must not be seen here in daylight.'

'Let's go up to the palms; I may be able to find where I slept.'

They hurried from the open sands, with all the time the light strengthening, and Jason saw that the two Japanese still wore their lightweight business suits and that Sumitomo carried a smart leather attaché case. They looked curiously formal against the background of palm and forest. He searched about, then darted forward. 'Here's where I slept – and look, here are my footprints and his!' There was his hollow, the sand still heaped up where he had burrowed into it. He showed Matsutan where he had forced his way through the wall of bushes and the three of them pushed through in under the trees. Outside it was now clear day, but under the trees it was still dark, and as they waited for the light to strengthen, Jason recounted the various moves in his first escape. 'There was a big tree,' he explained, 'a big white tree. I hid near it. After that I went uphill.'

'You ran to the tree from here?'

'Yes. It's not very far.'

He tried to imagine himself running again, racing through the trees to hide. He led the two Japanese back inside the edge of the trees, trying to remember just how far he had run. Then it had seemed miles – but suddenly he saw the tree, unmistakable with its huge buttresses and fine-grained whitish bark, and at the sight of it he again felt a twinge of remembered terror. Yes, there he had crouched, between those buttresses, and from it had crept away the few yards which had saved him.

Matsutan, seeing his expression, said: 'This is where you hid.'

'Yes. And here is the spur leading up to the ridge. The little camp is near the top, where a stream begins.' Jason was quiet now and confident. He made as if to lead but Matsutan stopped him. 'Please.' Sumitomo went in front, climbing carefully in his black leather shoes. He still looked formal, but he now carried a small automatic pistol in his right hand.

On and up they went, and Jason began to see how far he had actually gone in his flight. As the slope steepened towards the ridge, the morning sounds from the beach dwindled away. They climbed easily, moving with care for the thorn tendrils while all the time the forest gloom lightened, then Sumitomo stopped. The stream flowed in front of him, with the little camp beyond. Bundles of cut leaves, yellowing at the edges, still lay where they had been cast down, and the lean-to shelters were still half-finished, undisturbed except for one overturned. Sumitomo threw a quick, doubtful glance over his shoulder and shook his head.

With a gesture to Jason to stay still, Matsutan went forward beyond Sumitomo, his own pistol out. Gun-hand forward he edged through the camp, stood a long moment, turned and came back. He looked inquiringly at Jason, who searched behind the tumbled lean-to, found the blowpipe lying on the ground, lifted it and showed it to Matsutan. Sumitomo walked a few yards down the slope and looked about. 'There.' He pointed.

A muscular leg, the trousers rucked up to the knee, stuck out from behind a tree. They moved round, keeping their distance, and saw the dead hijacker lying propped between tree and slope, his left arm flung back, his right crooked in front of him. Matsutan stooped to examine the body, with Sumitomo standing on guard a yard or two away, and Jason, fearful yet fascinated, standing at the edge of the camp.

'He died by the dart.' Matsutan straightened up.

Jason forced himself to look at the man he had killed, and when he looked, he could not turn his eyes away. There was a faint bruise in the centre of the hijacker's forehead, his eyes were open and seemed to glare at Jason, and his lips were drawn back to show tightly clenched teeth. Gripped in his right hand was the snapped-off shaft of the dart, the delicate white wadding crushed and broken, and from his ribs protruded the broken shank, the head buried deep. His automatic still lay beneath him, and Matsutan identified it for Jason. 'Kalashnikov,' he said, 'Soviet.' He lifted the dead man's outflung hand. The finger-nails were dark with earth, and Matsutan pointed to a small patch of clawed ground. 'He did not struggle for long. That poison was quick. Are there any more darts?'

'There were some in a little basket.' Jason climbed up to the camp. In the centre of it lay the quiver of darts and he picked it up gingerly.

Back at the tree he found Sumitomo busy with equipment from the attaché case photographing and finger-printing the dead man, taking care not to touch the hand that clutched the dart, while Matsutan stood studying a folder, turning over sheets of photographs and descriptions till he stopped at one page: 'This one.' Jason peered over his shoulder. The sheet held a photograph surrounded by close-written ideographs in Japanese. Enlarged from a group picture of solemn-faced students, it was of a young man in his late teens or very early twenties, looking at the camera with earnest attention.

'Hirada Tosei,' said Matsutan, 'a student – a good student, at Keio University.'

Jason looked from the pleasantly serious face in the

photograph to the death-mask glaring at them from the slope of forest earth, and back at the file again. Matsutan sighed and clicked his tongue. 'Like so many, an idealist. He wanted to change the world.'

'But how – '

'How did he come to this?' Matsutan laughed shortly. 'First he joined the student groups who fight the police when political affairs do not please them. He also became increasingly deeply involved in radical politics. His studies suffered, he was warned to improve his work, but eventually had to leave the University. When approached by the radical Japanese Red Army, he was unemployed, had a reputation as a trouble-maker and was desperate.' He sighed again. 'The change did not take long – a few months, no more.' He pointed to the photograph. 'That was taken last year.'

'Finished.' Sumitomo was packing up his suitcase.

The two men began a low discussion in Japanese, and Jason guessed what they were saying: if the hijackers were told that their companion was dead, they would demand their revenge. Yet if they were not told, Sue and the other girl would die. Jason began to feel that this trip of theirs had been a waste of time. He should have spoken up to Colonel Chula last night and got it over. As it was he had just postponed the unpleasantness, whatever that was to be. If only, he thought, if only he could admit to killing the man, and then melt away into the forest like those aborigines. If *they* had done it, the hijackers could not call for blood.

He looked at the blowpipe in his hand, and round at the little camp. The aborigines ... A wild idea was beginning to form in his mind, an idea whose glimmerings came at the thought of the small brown men abandoning their camp and vanishing like shadows. His heart sank a little; the idea was too wild – no one would accept it; and yet . . . His eye fell on the neck of the dart, peeping from the wound in the dead man's ribs, his hand clutching the snapped-off shaft. He, Jason, had certainly not carried a blowpipe from the aircraft!

Matsutan was about to pull the Kalashnikov from under the hijacker when Jason said, 'Wait!' and the two Japanese looked at him in surprise. 'Don't move him,' he said, 'leave him, just as he is! Look!' He pointed at the dart and shook the blowpipe at Matsutan. 'Say we found him dead – say the aborigines were frightened by him, and killed him!'

Matsutan straighted up, staring at Jason, who repeated what he had said in case the Japanese had not understood. 'The aborigines have run away; no one knows who they are. Only they have blowpipes!'

'That is true. *You* did not bring it.' Matsutan spoke reflectively. 'It is a possible story – it is possible!' He spoke as if to himself, and Jason could see from his eyes that he was weighing up the probable reactions of the hijackers to the story. 'Like all idealists they have a strong feeling of persecution. They will suspect a trick. But,' he looked at the dead man, 'I do not see how else we can save innocent life.'

Jason shivered. Matsutan had not specified *whose* life.

'It would be better,' the Japanese detective went on, 'to have someone other than ourselves find him and carry him down. Perhaps we can ask Colonel Chula to, er, arrange a discovery.'

'Yes – but why carry him down?' Jason looked about. If Matsutan said it *might* work, it very probably *would*. How could they convince the hijackers beyond doubt? He was thinking out a likely sequence. 'Why not get one of them here?' he said eagerly. 'They can see this man just as he is, with the dart stuck in him. It's obvious nothing else killed him!' He saw a faint crease appear between

Matsutan's brows, and made himself speak more slowly. 'He has the bruise on his forehead,' he went on, indicating it and looking round at the Japanese, 'but he could have bumped against the tree when he fell! And all this,' he pointed to the yellowing leaf edges, 'they are not new, not made just now!'

Sumitomo was nodding his head slowly and Matsutan, eyes thoughtful and narrowed, looked from the body to the camp a few yards further up and then at the forest all round. '*Hai*,' he said decisively. 'It is a good suggestion.' He looked at Jason appraisingly. 'We will let one hijacker see the evidence – and form his own conclusions. We need explain nothing. He will see the obvious and will think the obvious. *Hai*,' he said again.

Then Jason had a sobering thought: 'They may not believe us. They may think it is a trick, and not send a man to look.'

'They will certainly think it is a trick,' agreed Matsutan, but added: 'They will also be very curious. Remember, they have been sitting there waiting for his return for a day and a night. They will also want to be sure that he is dead.' He spoke a word in Japanese to Sumitomo, who nodded agreement. 'In that period they must have also suspected that their comrade might have turned against them. These people suspect each other almost more than they suspect the police. That Rengo Sekigun purge and massacre of their own members on Mount Haruna showed that. No,' he said confidently, 'their own suspicions will make them send someone to look.'

Matsutan looked at his watch. 'It is nearly seven o'clock. If we are quick, we can be back before notice is taken of our absence. I will tell Colonel Chula where we found the body. He will not ask questions. I will explain that it would be best for a hijacker to see it. Let us go.'

Then he paused, the faint crease again appearing between his eyebrows. 'But why did this man follow you, Jason? Why was one boy important when they have many hostages?'

'I don't know,' confessed Jason. 'I've no idea. I think they were just angry that I escaped.' He was more immediately concerned with whether the hijackers would accept their story of the aborigines and the blowpipe. He held it up: 'They would not have left this behind.'

'You are right.' Matsutan looked around. 'It might not be safe to hide it here.'

'And the darts – we can't leave those either.'

'We will take them all down and hide them near the beach. Later we can cut them up and perhaps burn them. But we will leave his automatic. The aborigines would not have touched it.' He looked up at Jason. 'That will make it seem more natural. Now, we will run.' He removed his jacket and led off at a steady lope back down the spur towards the beach.

7

KIMONO

'HULLO, Jason – where've *you* been?' Deane, a mug of tea in his hand, was sitting yawning beside Bill at the wireless set. 'You must have been up since dawn!'

'I went to sleep too early,' Jason sat down. 'When I woke up, I couldn't go off again, so went for a trek along the beach. Thanks.' He took the mug of tea Bill passed him and sat sipping it, trying to look unconcerned.

'At least you look a bit better now than when we first saw you.' Michael Deane's blue eyes were suddenly sharp and observant. 'Then you looked rather like death – quite exhausted, and worried, too. That sleep has done you good, although' – and he looked at Jason carefully once more – 'you still don't look too easy in your mind. If anything's bothering you – '

'Everything's all right, thanks,' Jason replied hastily. 'I was just tired.' He took a deep breath, and to change the subject away from himself asked: 'Any news?'

'A lot went on while you were asleep – kept us up till after two. That's why we're still a bit bleary.' Deane blinked and rubbed his unshaven jaw. 'I'm afraid that the man who was stabbed died during the night, in spite of all that young medical officer could do.'

'The big man – ' Jason stopped. He found it difficult to go on.

'Only then did the hijackers bring him out. They're a wicked lot.'

They sat silent till at last Jason asked: 'Any news from outside? Anything about the demands from Israel?'

'First, there's a Thai Minister on the way down – he should be arriving by helicopter shortly – and a Japanese Minister is coming with him. The Japanese Government was dreadfully concerned over the Lod Massacre by Rengo Sekigun, and this threatens worse, if that's possible. There's no news from Israel yet – but the Thais here have had a demand themselves!'

'But the Thais have nothing to do with Israel!'

'Oh, this wasn't for the release of prisoners, this was for something much simpler – money, and a boat.' He smiled without humour. 'These boys have done their homework, all right. They handed over a letter, neatly typed out in quite good English, listing their requirements.'

'What did they ask for?'

'Curiously enough, not a great deal of money – the equivalent of only a hundred thousand dollars in yen and ticals. Other hijackers have asked for – and got – millions of pounds. They're being very modest.' He shook his head. 'It worries me. And remember, they've only asked for the release of six prisoners by Israel. That Black September gang who murdered the American Ambassador in Khartoum had asked for over a hundred.'

'What about the boat?' asked Jason. As soon as the sea came into things his interest was aroused.

'They knew exactly what the Thais have, and where. They've asked for one of the Thai Navy's fast patrol craft, a T-28. There's one in Songkhla, just up the coast.'

'Are they getting it?'

'Oh, yes! It's being loaded up with supplies and fuel.'

'And the cash?'

'Coming in by air from Bangkok.'

'That means they think they'll get their demands accepted!' Jason felt a surge of hope. The rights and wrongs of giving in did not trouble him; he thought only of the hostages.

'I wouldn't count on it.' Deane looked very grim. 'All reports indicate that Israel won't budge.'

'But surely it can't just do nothing!'

'Well, the Governments concerned are beginning discussions with Israel – '

'Beginning!' Mug half-way to his lips, Jason stared at him in astonishment. 'Only now! We were hijacked two days ago!'

'You were – but you must remember that your aircraft then vanished for a whole twenty-four hours.'

'What difference does that make?'

'It might have crashed, gone down in the jungle or into the sea. The hijackers' bombs might have gone off, or there might have been a fight in the air, and the crew disabled. Anything was possible.'

'But surely, during all that time – '

'I'll tell you what he means,' interrupted Bill bluntly.

'If your aircraft had just gone away and crashed somewhere, all those governments would have been relieved.
They'd have been let off the hook.'

'Never!' Jason forgot his own fears in total outrage. 'All
that time the rest of the world were just hoping we were
dead?'

'Not at all,' said Deane very seriously. 'People every-
where are very concerned indeed, and this hijack's the
lead story in almost all the countries outside the Soviet
block. Even China is running it. Unfortunately, this
hijack is an attempt to achieve a major defeat of Israel,
using the soft hearts of the West.'

'Well, they didn't choose much of a blackmail weapon.'
Jason spoke with puzzled irritation. 'One plane, only half
full, and nobody important on it. There aren't even any
Israelis! They've made a blunder there!'

'On the contrary – this was all deliberately planned,
very cunningly indeed. It's just – ' He broke off, 'Hullo –
what's going on?'

He got to his feet and strolled out from the group of
tents, gazing across at the beached aircraft. 'It's some sort
of discussion with the hijackers. Surely they're not making
more demands!' He took a pair of binoculars from the
case over his shoulder and looked through them. 'There
doesn't seem to be much happening.'

Jason felt his mouth go dry. With an effort he cleared
his throat and asked, 'May I have a look?'

'Sure!' Deane walked back to the tent and handed him
the glasses, a workmanlike pair of Zeiss five by eights. 'But
take care not to be spotted.'

A low sand ridge ran down to the promontory, and
Jason moved round and lay flat behind it and focused the
binoculars. Under the tip of the great wing stood two of
the Japanese hijackers, their Kalashnikovs levelled at a
small group standing at the edge of the roped enclosure. A

third hijacker stood back near the undercarriage, and the pale face of the fourth looked from a window of the first-class cabin. In the group Jason quickly identified the squat figure of Colonel Chula. With him were two un-armed Thai NCOs and Sumitomo, who was talking to the two nearest hijackers, punctuating each sentence with a slight bow. One hijacker was replying. He was tensed forward, his gun muzzle jerked angrily, and there was no suggestion of a bow. The man next to him – whom Jason recognized as the one who had worn the woman's clothing and had lost his wig – stood glowering, occasionally swinging the muzzle of his Kalashnikov across the little group in front, as if practising mowing them down.

Eventually the man behind called something and the two little groups facing each other stopped talking and stood in silence – the hijackers sullen and threatening, the Thais and Sumitomo in a passive, deliberately neutral pose – while he ran to the nose of the aircraft and called up. Jason held his breath and focused the binoculars on the shadows inside the forward door. There was a figure there, he could make out the shape, but the face – unnaturally pale, it seemed to him – remained indistinct.

'See anything much, Jason?'

'Won't be a minute.' Normally he'd never have dreamed of answering Deane's request so curtly but he could not let those binoculars go. The man calling up and the pale hijacker inside the forward door seemed to be having a protracted discussion; it went on and on, with Sumitomo and the Thais waiting patiently by the enclosure rope under the cameras of the journalists and the stare of the passengers at the windows. Eventually Jason handed the binoculars to Deane with an awkward apology: 'Sorry; I thought I'd manage to recognize the one in the front.'

Deane strolled out a yard or two, seated himself

comfortably on the sand ridge and, elbows propped on knees, held the binoculars steady to his eyes, while Jason, consumed with impatience, yet fearful of seeing Sumitomo and the Thais turned away, lay flat behind him.

'He's stopped his chat with the man inside,' Deane still held the binoculars fixed to his eyes, and Jason looked up. The third hijacker was walking swiftly back towards the two men under the wing.

By now the whole of the camp had gathered that something unusual was afoot, and the soldiers not on duty, the cooks and fatigue-men, the villagers with their parangs and hatchets – even the Thais with the stalls of fruit and tobacco and vegetables had paused in their business and were gazing down at the two little groups by the tip of the great wing.

At this range of just over three hundred yards, Jason could not see the expressions on the faces, but in the fierce morning sunlight and against the white sand background their movements were sharp and distinct. The two Japanese under the wing, with a threatening gesture of their Kalashnikovs, moved back at a call from the third man and stood listening, with an occasional turn of the head.

'Hullo!' exclaimed Deane. 'Look at that!'

One hijacker gave a stiff bow in the direction of the nose of the aircraft, marched towards Sumitomo and the Thais, stopped and spoke, then ducked under the rope.

'He's coming out!' Deane put down the binoculars in astonishment. 'What on earth's going on? And they're heading up this way! Quick, Jason – back inside the tent!'

Walking rapidly the little procession set out along the shore – Sumitomo and Colonel Chula in the lead, the two unarmed Thai soldiers next and the hijacker, gripping his automatic, following a few paces behind. As they passed below the tents, Jason peeped out under the canvas, and got a good view of the hijacker. It was the man who had been disguised as a woman. He passed so close that Jason lowered the tent brailing, fearing that somehow his gaze might project his animal fear and hate to the hijacker, and put him on his guard. When they had passed he lifted the brailing again and watched them stride along the beach.

'They're turning up towards the palms.' Michael Deane had his binoculars up again. 'Looks as if they're going right into the trees behind. What on earth can they be after?' With a flash of insight, he wondered aloud: 'Perhaps it's something to do with that bloke of theirs who's missing!' He called to Jason: 'You can come out now, they've gone off into the forest,' and when Jason appeared, he asked: 'Wasn't it somewhere along there that you were hiding?'

'Yes, about there.'

'Well, I daresay we'll find out the answer in due course. But who's this?' He gave an unobtrusive flick of the hand, Jason vanished back into the tent again and from inside heard Deane call out, 'Morning – do anything for you?'

'Hullo there; looks as if we've had some activity this morning.' The voice, breezy and confident, came clearly through the thin canvas. 'Thought perhaps you could give me some gen. Those Siamese policemen taking a couple of Japs along the beach – what are they up to, any idea?' The voice now came from a yard or two beyond the tent, and Jason heard the faintest edge in Deane's reply: 'I've no idea, I'm not supposed to have any idea and I don't think you're supposed to have any idea either. And I don't think I'd go much farther along that beach, if I were you. Colonel Chula would be very disappointed if he felt that his instructions on security were not being followed.'

'He needn't know anything!'| The voice was now friendly and conspiratorial. 'I'm just after a bit of background. And say, did I hear from one of the natives about there being a white boy here – from that plane?'

'You're from the journalist's compound, I take it. Would you mind telling me your name and your paper or agency?'

'You're not exactly helping the press, are you?' the clipped accent was not quite English and Jason tried to place it, but gave up as the voice, resentful, now, grew fainter. 'I've got a job to do here the same as anybody else! These Siamese cops have no legal right to put these restrictions on us. I came here looking for a bit of help from the British and what do I get – ' The voice stopped abruptly, lost in the swish and rustle of leaves, shouts in Thai and the thud of hurrying feet.

'That's got rid of *him*!' Michael Deane reappeared grinning. 'When those Thai sentries appeared, he was off like a shot.' But he quickly grew serious again. 'That won't be the last we'll see of him; he's a persistent beggar.'

'Who was he?'

'I think he's a chap called Bedford. I've seen him about before – the last time was when the Black September raided the Israeli Embassy down the road from us in Bangkok. Swarms of journalists there, of course, but he was one of the quickest on the scene. He's a freelance; sells his stuff to the highest bidder – and does pretty well out of it.' He looked at his watch. 'Time for a word with the Embassy. Bill!' he called out through the tent wall, 'You through?'

'Giving 'em a call now, Mike.'

'Coming.' Deane hurried out leaving Jason sitting on his folded blankets. For a minute or two he sat listening hopefully to the cryptic monologue as Deane listened, acknowledged, put a query, then listened again – but it sounded unexciting stuff, concerned with protocol and

Government cables. Trust officialdom to make even a hijacking sound dull!

For the first time since the walk on the beach the evening before, Jason sat with nothing to do, and in spite of himself his mind kept wandering away to the little group in the forest. They would now be half-way up that rising spur – more if they moved quickly. Another quarter of an hour, and they'd be looking at the man who lay clutching a spine of wood the size of a large toothpick. The kimono man would look for bullet-wounds, for any sign to indicate that his comrade had *not* been killed by aborigines. Apart from the bruise on the forehead, however, there was no wound, only the stump of dart-head buried in his ribs. Jason felt his confidence flowing back. It would be all right; nothing could go wrong.

'Mister Jason?' Footsteps crunched on the sand outside, there was a discreet cough and 'Mister Jason?' Matsutan asked politely again and, hearing no reply, pushed aside a corner of the door flap. He was about to speak when his eyes met those of the boy. He stopped and looked searchingly at Jason, and Jason sat looking back at the Japanese detective, his brief surge of confidence evaporated. Matsutan's voice, low and inquiring, had jerked him back to a certain moment in their examination of the hijacker's body, and again he saw Sumitomo crouched and busy. 'His fingerprints,' said Jason in a dull voice, 'his fingers will be all marked with ink.'

'Ha-ssu ...' Matsutan let out his breath in a hiss of concern. 'You are right.' The lines on his face deepened. 'That was an error. Usually when we fingerprint corpses they have no further part to play. This time it was different – as so much of this affair is different.' He repeated: 'That was an error.'

His words were formal, but the heavy grating tone struck home to Jason and, in spite of his preoccupation he felt a stab of sympathy. Here was someone who had not treated him with adult aloofness, who had not dismissed his suggestion to trick the hijackers as preposterous or childish, and who was risking reprimand – or worse – to try to help. He tried to reassure Matsutan just as he had tried to reassure himself. 'Perhaps Kimono will not notice!' and at Matsutan's fractional lift of an eyebrow: 'That was one of the two who were dressed in kimonos, as women.'

'Ha! So – if the other was in the forward part, this must be the one who killed the big Englishman!'

'Yes! Yes, that's right.'

'And you think of him as "Kimono"?'

'Yes, I do. I'd know him anywhere.'

'That,' said Matsutan, 'may be very useful to us. Now, when they return, I will photograph them from the tent as they approach along the beach.'

'But you have photographed them already!'

'That is so. But this time the man you call Kimono will be photographed apart from the other hijackers. He can be seen in an individual setting, and therefore can be more certainly distinguished from the others. As yet,' he added grimly, 'those others have not actually killed anyone that we can prove. He has.'

'Is he in your book of photographs?'

'Ah, you noticed that! Yes, I think I recognize him as one Kashigawa, another student.'

'Are they all students?'

'Perhaps not the leader, the man in the forward cabin. I have not been able to see his face. But I came this morning to see if you can help us further.'

'Yes?' For the moment Jason had forgotten his worries as to what Kimono might see or deduce in the forest.

'The hijackers began with five men – not many for a long operation, and they had over fifty hostages. Yet when just *one* hostage out of fifty escaped, they sent one of their own five after him – not only at the time of escape, but again the next morning. That single unimportant escaper was worth a considerable effort to silence. Why? Again,' Matsutan went on, 'they allowed a doctor on board – yet would not let him off. Why?'

After a moment or two Jason said: 'There must be something on board which they do not want mentioned.'

'Correct. But what is it? That is why I have come, to ask you once more about what you saw. There is a mystery here, a great mystery. We know their demands, yet they do not indicate how they will know that these demands have been met.'

'Surely by wireless! They will hear it on the news!'

'False news can be broadcast as well as true, Jason, and they know that. No, there is something else. I have a feeling that if we can find out why they hunted you, we may discover their secret. Now, let us go over what happened once again.'

So Jason repeated (for the umpteenth time, he felt) his story of the hijack – the turn south, the landing, the fight by the galley, the assault on the Captain and his own escape – and Matsutan listened with his eyes half-closed, signifying only by an occasional sharp glance that he was listening with intense concentration. As Jason finished his recitation the Japanese sighed. 'I have thought over everything you have told me, but can find nothing of unusual significance.'

'Hullo in there!' Deane called towards the tent. 'That expedition of Colonel Chula's is on its way back. I can see them along the beach! Keep under cover!'

'We can see from here.' Jason led Matsutan to the far end of the tent, lay down and lifted the bottom edge of the brailing and pointed. The figures along the beach were still some hundreds of yards away, and Matsutan grunted

'Camera,' sprang from the tent and in a few moments was back again, his Nikon slung from his neck and a telephoto lens case in one hand. Rapidly he unscrewed the camera lens, opened the case and from it took a telephoto attachment that looked to Jason like a squat black telescope. In the shaded tent its lens glowed blue with captured light. Matsutan gave a confident hiss as he set the range and checked shutter speed and aperture. 'First I will get him in the group with the others.' He stretched out on the ground and settled himself like a sniper, the canvas of the tent brailing draped over his head and concealing the lens, and Jason followed his example.

The figures along the beach were not walking in the neat formation in which they had set out. Leading came Kimono, walking very fast, automatic gripped under one arm, gradually drawing away from Colonel Chula and Sumitomo. Well back, just emerging from the line of palms, came the two Thai soldiers, carrying something bulky between them. Beside him Jason heard the subdued click of the shutter and the swift scrape of the ratchet as Matsutan advanced the film. Click-scrape, click-scrape, click-scrape – in all he took half a dozen shots then lowered the camera. 'Now I will wait till he comes nearer, for close-ups.'

In spite of Matsutan beside him, the curious Thai soldiers standing watching and the half-dozen or so diplomatic staff emerging from their tents to stare, Jason still felt a thrill of unease as Kimono strode on, and he wrinkled up his eyes as he peered out from under the concealing canvas, trying to read the man's face. It was set hard, the corners of the mouth turned down and the brows knitted fiercely. Occasionally his lips moved and Jason saw his teeth; Kimono was speaking to himself, and Matsutan said in confidential tone: 'He is annoyed.'

Kimono was now close to the tent. In a dozen strides he

would pass below it and next to Jason came the swift click-scrape of Matsutan's camera, while Jason stared at the man's expression. Matsutan's choice of words had not been very good: Kimono was more than annoyed, he was raging. His mouth still worked and spittle flecked the corners, and his legs drove violently down, each step spraying up sand. Yes, he was in a dangerous fury – but was it because there was no one available to feel his revenge? Or – and Jason's skin crawled – was it a sign that only production of the man's killer would prevent retaliation against the hapless prisoners? He barely noticed as Kimono stormed past towards the beached aircraft, nor paid much attention to the voices outside, till Matsutan said: 'Here is Colonel Chula and Sumitomo.'

Jason pushed himself up and followed Matsutan out into the bright sunshine. Colonel Chula, standing talking to Deane, gave him a fleeting but penetrating look, then turned back to Deane. Sumitomo bowed to Matsutan, said one word in Japanese, then turned to Jason. 'All is well!'

Jason took a long, deep breath.

'That man was very – ' Sumitomo hesitated, searching for the word, 'doubtful.'

Jason found his voice. 'You mean suspicious.'

'Ah-so: suspicious. When we spoke of the forest people, he at first treated it with contempt, but when he saw the huts, he was a little convinced, but not much.' Sumitomo pursed up his lips, as if remembering something unpleasant. 'When he examined the dead man, he was angry, but he could see he had been killed by that small dart.'

'His fingers!' broke in Jason, rubbing the tips of his own fingers, 'The ink!'

'He saw it – so I said quickly that the Thai police had taken the fingerprints while the hijackers were wasting time arguing whether to come to see. He became more angry. But one thing finally convinced him.' He smiled as if surprised at their luck. 'While he was searching around for evidence of some trick, he found a little pipe, very small. Then he knew that it was true that little men had been there.'

'Here is the body,' remarked Matsutan. 'They are taking it to the hospital tent – no doubt for examination.' The two soldiers struggled past, looks of extreme distaste on their faces. Jason looked without emotion. Could this flaccid heap of dangling arms and legs be the same muscular devil that had filled him with such stark terror in the forest? And that waxen face, the glare smudged into a look of faint surprise, should it not fill him with guilt, or at least with regret for a human life lost, and by his hand? But he felt only relief.

'The Minister arrived a short time ago, I must inform him of these developments – of *official* developments,' added Matsutan at the sudden flash of alarm in Jason's eyes. 'The terrorist died by a dart at the edge of a camp of aborigines – and that is just what I will say. Then I will accompany the Minister to the hospital tent, where the doctor will be carrying out his examination.' He gave Jason a short bow. 'Once that is finished we will return to the main task.'

The main task . . . Jason wandered out along the palm-line beyond the tents. It was safe there now, but his elation had been punctured by Matsutan's last words. The main task of freeing the hostages remained; this violent, terrifying interlude had been just that – an interlude, no more. But why had it happened at all? Hands deep in pockets Jason walked slowly on in the dappled sunshine below the palms. He reached the patch of bush where he had first crept through into the forest – now a wide gap, marked with trampled footprints. Why had he been hunted like a dangerous animal? He knew nothing special about the hijackers; he had told Matsutan everything that had happened, and none of it had struck the Japanese detective as of unusual significance.

He had walked far enough; there was now that wretched newspaper man to look out for as well. Jason turned and began strolling back towards the tents. Soon it would be time for Bill to take another call from Bangkok — yes, there he was, out checking his aerial.

Jason stopped short, and with his clenched fist struck his thigh in discovery and exasperation. He knew now what he had not told Matsutan; he had not thought it worth mentioning at first, and had then forgotten. But now he remembered. He began to run.

8

THE IPOH TREE

JASON hurried through the palms with one thought in his mind – he must tell the Japanese detective what he had remembered, and he must tell him at once; but Matsutan's tent was empty and Jason remembered with impatience that he had said something about taking his Minister to the hospital tent.

A small crowd of interested soldiers and police clustered near the entrance to the marquee so Jason slipped round and found himself at the back of a small group standing before a partially sheeted form on a raised stretcher. Colonel Chula was there, as were a Thai police officer in uniform, the Thai and Japanese Ministers, each accompanied by an official, and Matsutan and Sumitomo, with on the far side of the stretcher, white-coated and wearing rubber gloves, the Thai doctor who had treated his feet. Seeing this assemblage Jason realized that the Thai Government was making very sure that there would be no doubts or queries later about just what had caused the hijacker's death.

Jason craned to see – his feelings of initial revulsion conquered by a morbid fascination – and at last the doctor straightened up. 'This seems straightforward, Gentlemen,' he announced in his American accent. 'Initial examination, together with the circumstances reported, appears to indicate that death was due to poisoning by antiarin, introduced intramuscularly by means of a blowpipe dart of the type used by the Orang

Pangan forest people of this locality.' He waited patiently while the translation was made into Japanese, repeated one or two of the more technical phrases, and explained that Orang Pangan meant Pangan Man, a tribe of nomadic aborigines, groups of whom wandered the forests of North-East Malaya and the Isthmus of Kra.

'The Orang Pangan use two kinds of dart poison,' he continued, 'both based on the sap of the Pokok Ipoh – the Ipoh tree, its botanical name *Antiaris toxicaria*. This is also the famed Upas tree of Java, a name meaning blood-poison, about which many traveller's legends have been told. It is one of the largest trees in the forest, growing to a great height – well over a hundred feet – and is easily recognized by its grey-white bark and huge supporting buttresses.' In the pause for translation Jason thought back quickly to the huge white tree within whose buttresses he had first hidden – and where, indeed, he had just left the blowpipe and darts, so that they could easily be found again and destroyed. It was curious, he reflected, how he had sensed danger from it.

'The sap from this tree is itself a poison,' said the doctor, 'and will kill small animals, but when cooked together with the juice of the shoots of a wild plant locally named *gadong*, in botanical terms, *Dioscorea triphylla*, it becomes much more powerful, in particular when freshly made, when it resembles sticky black treacle. It is then exceedingly dangerous. The local people say that even a grain of it under the finger-nails will cause death.'

Here the Japanese Minister broke in with a question which his secretary translated: 'If so dangerous, how can these people handle it?'

'They acquire immunity, Sir, by handling these poisons from childhood. Also, it is surmised that such immunity is an inherited characteristic, through generations of forbears who have handled these poisons.'

At the translation the Minister nodded and sucked in his breath in acknowledgement.

'As to the strength of the poison,' the doctor went on, 'I can only say what I have heard. Till now I have not yet encountered a case of such poisoning, and assumed I never would, although I have always been interested in the native charms and poisons of our country.' Behind his rimless glasses his eyes glittered with professional enthusiasm. 'I was told, however, that an elephant struck by two *Ipoh gadong* darts would be dead by nightfall, and we must assume that a human struck by one would be dead in a few moments, especially if struck in the fleshy upper part of the trunk near the heart, as in this case.'

He said a word to the hospital orderly, who pulled the sheet aside. 'As you can see, Gentlemen, the head of the dart is embedded deeply in the lower section of the left breast, having penetrated between the ribs. It must have been propelled with great force, and probably from a short distance.' As the doctor paused for the translation, something made Jason turn his head. Two very sharp brown eyes quickly veiled themselves; Colonel Chula gave him a polite smile and turned casually away.

'The head of the dart has snapped off,' commented the Thai Minister. 'Why?'

'The jungle people nick the neck of the darts. If the shaft is pulled, it breaks and the head remains in the wound.' With a pair of forceps, the doctor tugged at the spike, but it did not move. 'There it would stay until its work was done. I will leave it for final extraction at the forensic laboratory.'

'There is no doubt, then, about the cause of death?' This was Colonel Chula, speaking in English.

'Very little. From the appearance of the facial muscles, and from other evidence, the symptoms indicating anti-arin poisoning are present – clonic spasms of the muscles, that is, convulsions' – and he indicated the smudging facial grimace – 'paralysis, and systolic arrest of the ventricles of the heart.'

Jason heard the medical jargon without comprehension. He only knew that death had been quick.

Again the Japanese Minister spoke, and at the translation Jason realized that here was a man who wanted all the answers: 'Was there any chance of saving this man's life?'

'I understand, Sir, that he was not found until the following day. Even if he had been found at once he would have required immediate professional attention, together with laboratory facilities, but this would have had to be within a few moments of wounding.' The doctor spread out his hands. 'In the forest such things simply do not exist.'

'In Japan we have a saying: "For every poison an antidote",' persisted the Minister. 'Does not such a thing exist?'

The doctor smiled. 'The list of antidotes is a long one, and I have no doubt the jungle people had some to hand. There is the juice of a wild fruit named *limau nipis* – a very acid, thin-skinned lime; another method is to induce the victim to swallow dry earth, and there must be others. In this case, however, the man who fired the dart had little intention of saving his victim, whom he would have regarded as a dangerous enemy. Normally they are a timid, peaceful people, and use their blowpipes only for hunting food. This man must have frightened them.'

'Ah-so.' The Minister bowed briefly and fell silent again.

'No more questions? Very well, Gentlemen – the body will be dispatched to the forensic laboratory at Bangkok for a full examination. My colleagues there will be most interested – most interested!'

As the watchers began to move out Jason caught Matsutan's eye and jerked his head. He waited at the back of the hospital tent and Matsutan and Sumitomo came round to meet him. 'So, Jason,' said the detective gravely, 'the doctor has confirmed what we told the hijackers. But you wanted to see me?'

'I've remembered something. But first, is there any news from Israel?'

'It is understood that their attitude remains unchanged.' Matsutan looked sombre and Jason felt his heart sink. He looked up at the sun. It was still early in the day, yet the heat lay on him like a blanket of lead. He wiped a bead of perspiration from his lip and Matsutan nodded at the action. 'It is oppressive. There is no breeze, which is unusual by the sea.' He looked tired, and Jason guessed that he had been busy with discussions till late the previous night, and had probably slept little before his early expedition into the forest. 'But what is this thing that you have remembered?' asked Matsutan. For a moment Jason felt diffident. Was he making something out of nothing? He could hardly fail to tell Matsutan now, however, so he said: 'It was to do with their wireless.'

'Go on, please.' Matsutan's eyes were suddenly attentive.

'You remember that I said they called the Captain to the flight deck?'

'Yes, I remember. That was when they struck him.'

'I did not tell you that they had themselves tried to operate a portable set under the wing.'

'No, Jason, you did not tell me that.'

'I'm sorry,' Jason was abashed for a moment, but from Matsutan's interest felt that perhaps he was not bringing up something of no importance, that perhaps there might be something in his idea. 'This set they had – and it was a big one, a large-size transistor – had a rod aerial. They were pointing it horizontally towards the ridge first of all, then trying it round up along the beach and then down, but always back towards the ridge. It was then I heard someone say they wouldn't get much reception here because we were in a pocket.'

Matsutan and Sumitomo listened with rigid attention.

'It was only then that they moved up to try the aircraft wireless on the flight deck,' said Jason. 'Then, as you know they called for Captain Chisholm, and afterwards, when he asked for something to do with the electricity supply, one of the hijackers struck him across the side of the head with the butt of his gun.'

Matsutan acknowledged with a quick narrowing of the eyes and said: 'There is something else?'

'The other crew officers thought that the Captain had been knocked silly, that he wasn't talking sense. Now I'm not so sure.'

'What did you hear him say, Jason?'

'That the station he tuned to was speaking Arabic.'

For a long moment Matsutan stared at Jason, then 'Ahhh!' he breathed. His whole posture relaxed, the tense lines on his forehead smoothed out, but his eyes glittered. 'Arabic; of course.' He murmured in Japanese to Sumitomo, and Jason saw his quick glow of comprehension. So – his information had been of significance after all, though exactly what it meant to the two Japanese he could not guess. Matsutan saw his bewilderment, and smiled a hard smile. It was the first time Jason had seen the detective pleased and confident since he had arrived.

'Jason, have you ever heard of an organization called Al-Fatah?'

The boy shook his head. 'Not that I know of.'

'Well, then – what about the Palestine Resistance?'

'Oh, yes – of course. They're against the Israelis.' He stopped, realization dawning.

'And Black September?'

'Everyone's heard of them! But do you mean –'

'*Hai!*' Matsutan's jaw clicked shut on the word like a trap. 'Terrorism now has world-wide links, and one close link is between Japanese terrorists and those of Black September, which we now believe to be a branch of Fatah. In what direction from us is that ridge, Jason?'

'West.'

'And in what direction lie the Arab lands?'

'Also west.'

'So, Jason?'

'They will receive their messages from an Arab station!'

'Correct. Unfortunately there are many stations broadcasting in Arabic.'

Jason felt his spirits sink again. It all seemed hopeless. Even if the hijackers *were* listening in to an Arabic station, what good would this knowledge do – even if the station could be identified?

'On the other hand,' went on Matsutan, 'not all stations belong to countries which favour Black September. Saudi Arabia, for instance, has a Royalist regime, and as such is opposed by these guerrillas – and the King of Jordan, of course, is their enemy.' He smiled without humour. 'The terrorists have mainly themselves to blame for some unpopularity – unwise of them, as there is justice in the Palestinians' case.'

'How can we find out?'

'You have a British signaller here from the Foreign Office. I think that he may help us.'

'Yes – Bill.' Quickly Jason led them round to the tent. Stripped to the waist and seated on an upturned box under the shade of a stretched-out groundsheet, Bill listened to Matsutan's theory.

'Fatah, eh? They used to broadcast from Cairo, on its home service – so many hours a week, then had a row with the Egyptian Government and moved.'

While Bill was talking, Michael Deane returned from the morning briefing in the main marquee, but before sitting down he pointed out to sea. 'Look there!' They followed his outstretched arm and saw on the horizon the grey shape of a small naval vessel. Even at this distance, they could see that she was coming up fast, the bow-wave high and the faint trail from the single smokestack flattened out astern. 'It's *Chanthara*,' explained Deane, 'the Thai Navy's survey ship. She's been travelling all night from Bangkok at full speed.'

'A survey ship?' Bill looked puzzled for a moment, then his brow cleared. 'I get it: communications!'

'You're right.' Deane nodded. 'She's got the latest U S teleprinter stuff on board, and can transmit and receive on international frequencies at a tremendous rate.'

'It'll take the strain off these Thai Army signallers here,' said Bill with feeling. 'They're swamped with incoming stuff – and outgoing, too. I don't think one of them's had a minute off since they arrived.'

'Where's the boat the hijackers asked for?' Jason was impatient to see it arrive; the sooner it came, the better – it might just give them the idea of leaving!

'It should be here soon too,' said Deane. 'I expect they've been busy taking the guns out of her. *That* wasn't in the demand, so they're not being sent!' Then he looked round the little group: 'Been having a meeting of your own?'

'There's a suggestion that they may be listening to one of the Arab stations,' said Bill, and explained.

'H'm – sounds possible. But Arabic! These blokes can't even speak English!'

'Mr. Matsutan here suggests we listen and find out.'

'Even if you find the frequency, can you receive it with this set? Remember that's what gave the hijackers their trouble!'

'Ah,' said Bill with a faint grin, 'they relied on a rod aerial, and they had it stuck under the end of the wing. We've got something a little better than that,' and he nodded to his long, high aerial of copper wire slung between two palms.

'But there used to be dozens of these clandestine stations. How will we know which it is?'

'Easy enough,' said Bill, 'there's now only one. For years the guerrillas, the fida'i, had bases in a number of Arab countries, from which they broadcast. These stations all had impressive names – Voice of the Storm, Voice of Fatah, Voice of the Palestine Liberation Organization Central Committee and so on. But after a spot of bother with their hosts, they decided to amalgamate into one, which they called the Voice of Palestine.'

'That might be the one we're looking for!' Jason was fired by excitement. 'It *must* be, if the hijackers are listening for an Arab station!'

'If you knew how many other stations broadcast in Arabic you wouldn't be so sure.' Bill made a wry face. 'The Russians alone broadcast in Arabic for hours every day of the week; then there's Sudan and Somalia, as well as the Arab countries themselves. All of them are engaged in the feud with Israel.'

'And I'll tell you another that broadcasts in Arabic,' broke in Deane, 'Malaya – that's south, of course. They've just begun a new Arabic service.' He nodded to Jason. 'I think that the terrorist link is our strongest bet, though God knows what we'll find out from it. I shouldn't think there's an Arabic speaker this side of Kuala Lumpur!'

'We'll just have to listen,' said Bill. 'But there is one other point that suggests this station.'

'What is that?' Matsutan had listened to the rapid, rather colloquial English with strained attention, and seeing his expression, Bill slowed his speech. 'The hi-jackers are demanding that the released men be put across the border into Syria.'

'Syria is the natural choice,' said Matsutan. 'It is very hostile to Israel, unlike Jordan or Lebanon.'

'That clandestine station is also in Syria.'

'Are you sure?' It was Deane. 'I thought that when Cairo and other transmitters closed down, it couldn't be located.'

'It was located all right, and it was the station's own fault.' Bill laughed. 'Last year we were listening to a re-cording of one of its broadcasts – about March, I think it was – when we heard them go off the air with a shout of "Zionist air raid!" and the sound of bombs going off. Well, that day the Israelis made only one bombing raid – on a fida'i base just north of the town of Dar'a, in south-western Syria.'

'There's still the puzzle about the language,' said Deane. 'That just doesn't fit! We mustn't think of this as anything more than a long shot.'

'We'll have a listen, anyway,' said Bill. 'I'll get on to Bangkok and get them to find out its frequency and broadcasting times.'

'How long will this take?' asked Matsutan.

'We should get the information of the station frequency quick enough. I used to know it myself; it's somewhere up in the nine hundred kiloHerz, I think. But I've got to get it accurately or we'd just be wasting our time. What may delay us is the broadcast timings.'

'Why?'

'Except when there's something afoot, these clandestine stations don't usually put out anything during working hours. They'll do maybe an hour before their target audi-ence sets off for work in the morning, and then perhaps an hour at midday, when they're eating their meal and maybe listening to their transistors, and possibly again at night. We must remember, too, the difference in times of day.' He looked at his watch. 'Anyway, I'll try and get the details from control now, and I'll give you a shout as soon as I hear.'

Matsutan rose, with Sumitomo, and they bowed formally. 'Thank you!' Then he said to Jason: 'I am going to examine the aircraft from the rocks. I think it may be safe for you to come, if you like.'

'Thanks.' Jason jumped up. 'There isn't anything else we can do that might help?'

'We must just wait in patience.'

Jason and the two Japanese went to the promontory, keeping in the dead ground behind it till they reached the cover of the rocks. Matsutan was slung about with camera and binocular cases, and when he had chosen an observation point where two boulders sloped up together, he took from one case a pair of binoculars of a size and power that made Michael Deane's old five by eights seem like a toy. He lay flat, edged himself up, focused the lenses and lay for some moments, examining the beached aircraft and occasionally muttering a word to Sumitomo. At length he lowered the binoculars and handed them to Jason. 'Here, Jason – you look now.'

The tide was ebbing, and he saw the two children playing on the sand, the stewardesses and other women passengers with them. It seemed ludicrous that they should be in instant danger of being blown up or burned alive because of unresolved quarrels thousands of miles away. It was more than ludicrous: it was horrifying. He swung the binoculars. There were two of the hijackers resting in the shade of the wing, and the third man seated propped against one of the great tyres of the undercarriage. The fourth man, the white-faced leader, was still out of sight up on the flight deck. Because of them the parents were frantic and those little children might die horribly.

'There is no more to find from here.' Matsutan carefully wound the strap round the binoculars and put them away. 'Now we must wait for the reply from London. There is nothing else we can do.'

Jason stifled a yawn. The rocks were warm with the sun, he had been up early and his immediate tension had been released by the hijackers' acceptance of the death of their comrade. He settled down lower, where sand had drifted between two boulders, and blinked sleepily at Matsutan. The detective looked at him narrowly. 'Do not sleep, Jason,' he warned. 'If you sleep now, you will lie awake tonight and be weary again tomorrow – and,' he added in a significant tone, 'who knows what tomorrow will bring?'

Jason rubbed his face and eyes and stifled another yawn. Matsutan was right, of course; to sleep now would be a great mistake.

'Why do you not swim?' suggested Matsutan in his curt English. 'You can remain on this side of the rocks.'

'Good idea – might wake me up!'

Quickly Jason stripped off his olive-green shirt and trousers. With the tide ebbing, the sea was shallow off the rocks but the three feet or so of water gave him enough depth for a long, shallow dive, and the clean sting of sea-water woke him at once. He surfaced, took a great breath, and dived again, noticing as he did so that the two Japanese, who had been watching him, had turned and were looking back at the beach. Something, some instinct, warned Jason to be cautious. He turned under water and let himself drift up behind a rock.

Not ten yards away Matsutan was speaking, his voice curter than ever. 'You cannot stay here, please,' and Jason heard a persuasive voice reply, a voice that was not quite English: 'It's quite all right, I'm a correspondent – '

'No! I beg pardon!' Matsutan, his voice angry, was beginning to lose control of his English, but Jason did not notice. He had heard that other voice an hour ago, through the tent canvas. It was Bedford, the freelance journalist, and he remembered Deane's comment: ' – a persistent beggar'. Jason edged further out of the water and put an eye round a rock.

The journalist was little taller than Matsutan, but he was thicker-set and much heavier, and perspiration gleamed through his thinning fair hair. Slung from his shoulder was a zip-fastened leather case and he carried a small camera slung round his neck. In front of him Matsutan stood to attention, body courteously bowed, but his neck was flushed and Jason saw that he was tense and angry. Sumitomo stood to one side, making no attempt to speak or interfere, almost as if he were waiting for some familiar occurrence.

'I'll just have a word with that boy who was in swimming,' said Bedford, making as if to pass.

Matsutan took a long pace backward and bowed again. 'Please,' he said. Whether Bedford mistook the Japanese detective's meaning or whether he decided simply to ignore him Jason could not tell. What he did see was Bedford, smiling, begin to walk round Matsutan. The Japanese waited a fraction till the other's nearest foot bore his weight, then slid his own foot against it, seized Bedford's shirt by sleeve and collar and pulled sharply forward and down across his own bent thigh – all in one swift, easy movement which deposited the journalist with a bump on the rocks, facing back the way he had come. Jason blinked. Matsutan once more stood at attention, bowing slightly as if he had never moved.

For a moment the journalist sat there, then slowly got

to his feet and brushed grains of sand from his trousers. 'Judo, eh?'

Matsutan said nothing, and Bedford, looking angrily from him to Sumitomo, turned away, jumped down on to the wet sand and walked quickly across the beach and into the palms, well clear of the tents and the eyes of the Thai sentries.

'That's got rid of *him*!' Jason pulled himself from the water up on to the rocks, looking at Matsutan with a new respect. That swift, easy movement had not only stopped the journalist in his tracks; it had made him look undignified without hurting him – and was an unmistakable warning to stay away lest worse befall him. 'You must be good at judo!'

'It was a simple throw,' said Matsutan, dismissing the incident, but Sumitomo murmured to Jason: 'Mr. Matsutan is a Black Belt, seventh Dan.'

But the older man's expression did not reflect Jason's relief. 'He will try again, that journalist, but in another way. He is no fool.' At the boy's raised eyebrows he explained: 'If he were stupid, he would have tried to bribe me, or to push past again. He was quick, and changed his mind at once. We must be careful, for what he sees will be announced to the world.'

'And get back to the hijackers!'

'Yes, for they will listen to Tokyo's radio world service in Japanese, for sure.'

Jason was wide awake. The sea-water, the quick alarm at Bedford's approach, the rush of relief at Matsutan's swift and confident handling of an awkward little situation, all made him forget his earlier drowsiness. In spite of the fierce heat of the sun Jason felt fresh, impatient for action. He clambered higher up on the rocks and looked cautiously over at the aircraft. Perhaps it could be rushed! He visualized the hijackers under the wing being shot down; a quick rush by the Thais, the passengers jumping down into the water ... They might just get clear before Speedwing II caught fire. From outside it looked deceptively easy, but inside ... He remembered the long rows of seats, and pictured the scrum of bodies piling up in the gangway if someone tripped. And if the stewardesses did not first get to the children – no, it wouldn't do.

'Mr Deane is waving to us.'

At Sumitomo's call Jason eased himself back down and looked towards the tents. The tall figure was waving an arm from side to side over his head to attract their attention, and when he saw them turn to face him, he beckoned urgently.

'They've heard something! Come on!' Jason led off for the tent at a run.

9
THE KEY

'HERE'S the reply!' Bill held out the message pad and Jason listened tensely as Matsutan read out in his careful English. 'Your station Voice of Palestine Liberation transmitting on 928 kiloHerz stop scheduled casts 0430 to 0530 GMT and 1300 to 1400 GMT daily stop unscheduled casts have been logged at 0800 1000 1200 and 1600 GMT daily since second Jan stop repeating pattern previously observed during anti-Israel operations now transmitting news and patriotic music only message ends.'

'What's our GMT here?' Deane's question brought a nod from Bill. 'You mean, which of these casts can we listen to first?' He looked at his watch. 'It's gone eleven Bangkok time, and we're seven hours ahead of GMT. We might hear something in half an hour.'

'Can we make a tape?'

'Sure,' replied Bill to Matsutan's query. 'There's a linked recorder in the set. Do you want me to tape the whole cast, or switch on when you think you've got something?' For a few minutes they discussed technicalities, and finally Bill said: 'That's it, then. Now we wait.'

'Come on,' said Deane, 'it's more than time for elevenses. We'll knock off for a bit and sit in the shade. It's murder under this awning.' He led off up to the palms, and the Thai orderly brought them cups of pale green tea. The English lay sprawled untidily, tasting the unfamiliar brew doubtfully, while the two Japanese hitched up the knees of their trousers, tucked their heels beneath them and sat neatly on the ground, sipping at the pale tea and breathing out in audible appreciation.

'Not exactly sergeant-major's tea, is it?' commented Bill. 'Gosh, it's hot – the weather, I mean. Feels like an oven.'

Deane wrinkled his brows: 'It's unusually sticky. Beginning to feel a bit thundery. A good shower of rain'd do us a lot of good.' He mopped his face. 'Ah, *Chanthara*'s arrived.' They watched as the ship dropped anchor out in deep water, and a boat was lowered and headed for the beach.

For a short while, they sat in silence under the palms, isolated from the busy noises of the Thai camp only two hundred yards away, with occasionally the swelling racket of a helicopter setting itself down and taking off again. They had little to do until the time came to test out the fragile theory of some clue emerging from the ether to help them free the imprisoned hostages. The actual nature of their gaolers – possibly their executioners – seemed a mystery, and Deane said curiously to Matsutan: 'Why are Japanese involved in a quarrel about Palestine? Surely it must be meaningless for them!'

'The Palestine question is not considered meaningless by the Rengo Sekigun.' Matsutan paused in reflection, as if unsure how to explain, and went on: 'It is considered by them to be part of a world-wide revolutionary struggle to overthrow established governments.'

'But why do they go abroad?'

'They feel they achieve more by violence abroad, although in Japan they have had many violent encounters with authority. In June 1970, for instance, no less than nine members of this organization hijacked a Japan Air Lines airliner. They did not use guns, but Samurai swords, and they forced the pilot to fly to North Korea. Those nine are still there, studying revolutionary tactics.'

'Maybe some of this lot – ?'

'No, I do not think so.' Matsutan shook his head decisively. 'We suspect that those nine will be kept for use against Japan itself.'

'Please go on.'

'It is often forgotten that the members of Rengo Sekigun are mainly students from middle-class, sometimes wealthy homes. This presents a serious danger.' Matsutan spoke with care. 'The Japanese Government fears that if such men were to fall under the control of professional criminals, they would become a great menace.'

'But is this likely to happen?'

'I fear so. We captured the leader, Tsuneo Mori, and four others in the mountains north of Tokyo, after a ten-day siege, and he hanged himself in his cell.' Matsutan grimaced. 'That provided us with yet another worry – who will take over the leadership?'

'And you fear that this will fall into the grasp of a professional criminal?'

'We fear it greatly. But to continue. From Mori's confession we knew that the original strength of this organization had been some fifty-five members. Of these nine had fled to North Korea; fourteen, whose graves we then found, had been done to death by their companions for various failings – including one girl revolutionary who had committed the serious bourgeois crime of wearing ear-rings – and five we had captured. That made a total of twenty-eight. We suspected that up to a dozen others, in fear of similar execution, had fled to the Tokyo slums, but we also suspected that several remained active. To our shame and sorrow we were proved right. Two months later three members of Rengo Sekigun travelled as tourists to Israel. There they carried out a massacre of passengers at Lod Airport, near Tel Aviv, killing twenty-four people and wounding seventy-four others. Two of the Japanese terrorists were killed and the third captured. This brought to thirty-one the known members of Rengo Sekigun definitely accounted for; over forty, if we include those who had fled.'

'And now we've found another five of the remainder.'

'Not so. Only four.'

Deane looked surprised. 'There were five hijackers!'

'*Hai.*' Matsutan nodded. 'I have identified four – first the dead man, Tusei; then Kashigawa – whom Jason calls Kimono – and, by observation through field glasses, the other two. All four were on our files. But the fifth man, one of the two who wore women's clothing and who is still on the flight deck, I have not yet seen. And he is the leader of *this* group, at least.'

'You suspect that he may be a professional criminal?'

133

'*Hai*,' Matsutan spoke with conviction. 'Why is he the only one who has kept himself hidden from our cameras and binoculars?'

'But what advantage will he gain if he succeeds?'

'Whoever he is, he will become the undisputed boss. His organization will gain many new, ardent recruits. At one stroke he will become master of the most feared organization in Asia. Remember, for the sake of the revolution these young men will do anything – anything.' He hesitated once more. 'I did not mention this earlier, but it is as well to know, and indicates their mentality. One of the men executed had been done to death by his own two brothers – all in the name of the revolution.'

Jason sat silent. His earlier exuberance had faded through this long catalogue of horrors, and in spite of the glaring sunshine he felt that he sat in a cold shadow, a shadow which lay across every soul in that aircraft.

'Do you have any idea who this man might be?'

'There is a certain Fukuda, a gang boss in the Tokyo area. We have heard little of him for some months. He is an experienced and ruthless criminal, certainly capable of this action.'

'Any others?'

Matsutan hesitated: 'There is one Yasuno, from Iyo Prefecture, a man of no great stature in the criminal world. But both Sumitomo and I consider him a likely candidate.'

'Why is that?'

'He is ruthless and ambitious, but so far his ambitions have been frustrated by other gang bosses with more powerful organizations than his own.'

'In that case surely he does not have the required ability,' said Deane.

'There are two reasons why other criminals have

tended not to group with this man, thus giving him that appearance of weakness. First, he is a man of some education, and was therefore felt to be aloof. Second, he is still young, under thirty.' Matsutan smiled. 'In Japan even the criminal classes have a decent respect for age in their hierarchies. But,' – and he looked grim again – 'Yasuno's youth and education would make him appeal to student revolutionaries, as if he were one of themselves.'

'But this is just a guess.'

Matsutan nodded, with a slight bow from his hips as he sat. 'Just a guess. If the man in that aircraft is careful, we will never find out.'

'Here's the hijackers' boat!' Heads turned as Jason pointed. Round the next headland came a long, sleek launch, bow-wave creaming, and they stared as it roared across their front.

'She's big!'

'Yes, Jason, she's big, all right. I've seen these before, up by Bangkok – twin-shaft diesels, twenty tons displacement, crew of five – ' He broke off. 'Of course! There were originally *five* hijackers, weren't there!' He walked out with his binoculars and stood studying the scene beyond, giving a commentary for Jason's benefit; 'Hove to just beyond the aircraft – down anchor – engines off – ' then added: 'They're not wasting much time handing her over. Those hijackers have got a man out already.'

'Yes.' Matsutan had his binoculars trained on the launch. 'That is one Hara. He is known to be good with engines. All, of course, are used to the sea.'

'Soon be time to listen to that station,' Bill called out, and they hurried back to the awning. He put on the headphones, switched on, spun the dials till he reached the frequency and made a face. 'Heavy interference.' He took off the headphones, laid them on top of the set and turned up the volume, and the listening men heard the hiss and crackle of static.

'I'll plug in a spare set of 'phones.' He looked round the group inquiringly, the spare headphones in his hand, then offered them to the Japanese detective. 'You'd better have these, Mr Matsutan. You know more what you're looking for!' He looked at his watch: 'If we're going to get the station, we should hear something in under forty seconds. They're usually pretty punctual.' He left his own headphones upturned on the set, and Matsutan stood holding the spare set slightly away from his ear.

Jason looked round the tense little group. He felt little real hope, the comparison was so grotesque. On the one hand the governments of great powers were desperately trying to find some acceptable solution; on the other four men of little rank – and a boy – were crouched round a wireless set on a remote beach, groping among the air waves for a key which, even if it existed, they were not sure they would recognize.

'Carrier wave!' Bill touched a dial, then: 'Here we are!'

A blare of music sounded faintly through the crackle; it faded as a voice took over and Bill slapped his knee. 'Got it!' The five heads bent round the set, and from the two sets of headphones a voice sounded, the words harsh and strange in their ears: '*Sawt al-Filistiniyah!*' it proclaimed, '*Sawt ath-Thowrah al-Filistiniyah!*' Again the martial music broke in, died away and was replaced by the rapid gutturals of Arabic. The listening men looked at each other and Deane shook his head. 'Doesn't sound like our thing at all.' Again came a burst of martial music, followed by the announcer's voice: '*Sawt ath-Thowrah al-Filistinyah!*'

'He's making sure we know what station it is,' commented Bill. 'A bit unusual.' Again came the rolling

Arabic phrases and Bill said, 'That'll be the news – there'll be several minutes of this before whatever else they've got in the programme.' He made a fractional adjustment to the tuning dials and sat back, but Matsutan stood doggedly with the headphone clamped against one ear as the long minutes ticked past.

Bill looked at his watch. 'The news'll be ending in a moment.' He adjusted the frequency slightly as the rapid Arabic faded and it became clearer. The news reader's voice stopped, again came the announcer's call-sign: *'Sawt al-Filistiniyah ...'* It stopped, but instead of the martial music there was a silence. Bill leant forward to the set, but before his hand reached the tuning dial, a new voice sounded, a deeper voice in different curt tones. Eyes blazing, Matsutan struck Sumitomo's shoulder and the three Englishmen looked from the set to the Japanese. The strange voice seemed to be repeating two or three phrases again and again. Then there was a pause and the announcer broke in once more with: *'Sawt al-Filistiniyah ...'* Matsutan lowered the headphones from his ear and Bill switched off the set.

Matsutan spoke in a triumphant hiss, and the listening Englishmen again heard the phrases that had crackled through the headphones:

' *"Nigitazu ni,*
    Funanori sento." '

Crouched by the tape recorder Sumitomo also wore a look of triumph, his teeth showing in a fierce smile.

'You've got something!' Jason felt a surge of hope.

'Not much, Jason, but something. That was a recording of a Japanese voice. I will tell you what it said:

"Here at Nigitazu,
    We wait to put to sea." ' He looked round the tense faces. 'By itself that means nothing, but from its phrasing it sounds like part of a thirty-one syllable *tanka*.'

'Does it have any hidden meaning?'

'No, Mr Deane, but I think I understand its purpose. It is the first half of a message. That *must* be what the hijackers are listening for!'

'Sounds like it, all right,' said Deane thoughtfully. He repeated the two lines,

' "Here at Nigitazu,

"We wait to put to sea." That describes their situation, doesn't it? They've got that launch out there, and as soon as they hear their demands have been accepted, they'll be off, out to sea!'

'I think, however, that those two lines mean only that nothing has yet taken place,' said Matsutan in his careful English, and Sumitomo nodded agreement. 'But – what is the phrase that will tell them that their demands have truly been met?' He looked round the circle of intent faces. 'Surely it will be the next syllables of that same *tanka*? The station will have it recorded, and will play it as soon as the prisoners arrive safely in Dar'a.'

'Do you know the next syllables?'

'Alas, I am no scholar. I know a few *tankas*, as do most Japanese, but there are so many . . .' Matsutan gave an apologetic duck of the head.

'Even if we did know it,' said Deane with a sigh of resignation, 'there isn't much we could do about it. We couldn't exactly ask the Palestine Resistance to broadcast it for us!'

'We could broadcast it ourselves.'

At Bill's interjection Deane looked at him sharply. 'What do you mean?'

'This machine transmits as well as receives, you know.' Bill tapped his wireless set. 'If it's just a case of bamboozling these characters in the aircraft, I think we could do it with this equipment we've got here.' With the others gazing at him, he explained: 'If we can find the rest of that bit of poetry, or whatever it is, Mr Matsutan here could record his own voice, and I'd transmit it on the same frequency, about ten seconds before the other crowd begin *their* transmission and crowd them out. We could tape the whole of their broadcast in Arabic, dub in Mr Matsutan's voice – with plenty of static – and give it to them from four hundred yards as against four thousand miles.'

For a moment there was dead silence, as the simplicity and audacity of Bill's scheme sank in. 'It's risky,' said Deane.

'Is Israel going to hand over those terrorists?'

'I don't think so.'

'What will those Rengo Sekigun do when they realize that?' Bill looked round the silent faces. 'See what I mean? Unless we come up with something, those people in the aircraft are going to burn in front of us.'

'You are right,' said Matsutan decisively. 'But this is also a very dangerous thing to do, for if they think they are being tricked, they will blow up that aircraft in our faces.'

'And themselves too?' objected Deane. 'Surely not!'

'You must realize that these men are Japanese.' Matsutan's voice was very grave. 'They consider themselves as soldiers in a war of revolution. Like our soldiers of the Emperor in the wars of the past they consider death as lighter than a feather but duty as heavier than a mountain.' He turned to Jason. 'You know the phrase "Kamikaze". Although dishonourable, these terrorists will behave with the same determination. They will stand under the fuel tanks as they blow them up. In fact,' he gave a heavy sigh, 'I fear that some of them would prefer a public death – one watched by the world – to success with their demands.'

Jason thought back to the hate-filled face of Kimono, and shivered.

'At least let us try to discover the remaining syllables of that *tanka*,' said Matsutan. 'I will request the Minister's permission to ask the Embassy. There are scholars enough there!'

'Whatever you do, don't ask by wireless,' said Bill. 'Other people besides ourselves listen – people who may not want things to work out. Send it by that survey ship's teleprinters. It's very quick, and they encode and decode automatically.'

'Of course. Colonel Chula will, I think, allow such a message. Also,' he pointed out, 'I must inform the Minister of these developments, even though he is so busy with diplomatic pressures.' He hurried off, and in a few minutes he returned. 'All is arranged.' He smiled. 'The Minister was surprised. Colonel Chula was also greatly interested, but I do not think he sees this puzzle as helping to solve our difficulty here.'

The little group relaxed, idly listening as Bill tuned his set. The immediate tension had left them, and Jason began to feel that they were busy on a wild goose chase. It all seemed so improbable, so dream-like. He wiped his face. It was hot! He'd resume his interrupted swim – that would cool him off and help to pass the time till some sort of answer arrived from the Japanese Embassy in Bangkok. He was about to tell Deane where he was going when a babble of voices in Thai broke out beyond the line of palms, and they jerked round to see a figure vanish into the trees and a Thai sentry running along the beach, waving and calling.

'What was that!' Matsutan jumped up. In a moment or two the sentry turned back and came towards them. He spoke in Thai, angrily, his outflung arm pointing up to the trees. When he saw that they did not understand he touched his hair and pointed to Deane's fair hair and back up to the trees again.

'A European in the trees.' Deane nodded and the Thai continued his mime. He put both hands to his chest, a few inches apart, lifted them to his face, closed one eye and pressed down several times with his right forefinger, then pointed back to the trees again and moved his arms as if running.

'A European took several photographs and ran back into the trees!'

The Thai indicated a camera again, then made a big circle with his fingers.

'A big telephoto lens!' Bill looked concerned. 'Whoever it is has got us all individually in close-up, round the set.'

'It's that confounded journalist!' Deane was furious. 'If he can get that film out, he'll scoop everyone else. Those photographs, syndicated to the world press, will bring him in hundreds, maybe thousands of pounds.'

'More than that.' Matsutan spoke with curt anger. 'Published in Japan they will be reported by Tokyo radio – and my face is known. The presence of a European boy will also be mentioned in broadcasts – and who else could it be but Jason, who escaped from the aircraft? And we are listening to a wireless set! What will it mean to those in the Palestine Liberation Front when they hear?' He clenched his teeth. 'If we cannot recover that film and silence that journalist we may as well forget our attempts to deceive these hijackers.'

'Come on.' Deane sprang up. 'We'll go and see Colonel Chula – he's the only man who can help us with this.'

'Yes.' Colonel Chula put down his cheroot with a decisive gesture. 'If he has been in this restricted area without permission I can detain him, and have his film examined.' He gave a brief order, an office orderly seated in the corner jumped to his feet, listened, acknowledged with a word and hurried out.

'The sentry who saw him will fetch him.'

'Thank you.' Matsutan bowed, but before they left Deane asked: 'What news, Colonel — anything from *Chanthara*?'

'Much diplomatic activity, but little result.' He ground out the stub of his cheroot, and Deane saw the piled ash-tray.

'Something is wrong, Colonel?'

'We may not have much longer. The fatigue parties carrying supplies to the enclosure, and the sentries, report that the hijackers are getting restive.'

'And they will hear from Tokyo radio that there is no progress in the discussions,' said Dean. 'But at least they have not yet announced a deadline.'

'They will soon. When they do, I fear that they will keep to it.' Colonel Chula leant back in his chair, studying the two men in front of him. From outside the busy sounds of the camp drifted in to them — the chop of wood, voices in Thai, signallers in the communications tent calling, the chug of generators — and at length he asked: 'How is that boy? I think it may be time to send him home.'

'Yes,' said Deane, 'so do I. He doesn't say much and he does all he can to help, but I think he feels very badly about the people in the plane.'

'He had better leave before he sees — anything happen. He is brave, but he can do no more for us. And I really have little faith in this broadcasting trick the English sig-naller suggests. It is clever, but,' Colonel Chula shook his head slowly from side to side, 'if anything goes wrong — '

They looked round at running feet. The orderly, fol-lowed by a Thai soldier, saluted at the entrance, the ord-erly gasped out a sentence in Thai, and Colonel Chula flushed, and Michael Deane saw his fist clench on the table. He took a deep breath and said: 'The journalist has gone. He left a few minutes ago in a small fishing boat —

and I cannot spare men or boats to go chasing him.' He smiled angrily. 'The only boat not busy is the hijackers' T-28.'

'Which way did he go?'

'South. He will head for Kota Bahru – it is outside my jurisdiction.'

'When will he reach it?'

'These sailing boats can do up to seven knots. He could reach Kota Bahru before midnight.'

'And his story will be flashed world-wide the moment he gets there.'

'That settles it.' Colonel Chula stood up. 'The boy must leave at once, and be clear of Thailand tomorrow.'

DECISION AT FIVE

EYES half-shut Jason was floating in the shallow sea, feeling the sun dry off each slap of water over his chest, when the Thai orderly came running down to fetch him. 'Colonel Chula,' he announced, pointing up towards the headquarters marquee. 'You,' and he beckoned.

Jason rolled over and jumped up, wiping the water from his face and eyes. Perhaps something had happened, some new development – maybe even the answer to that strange Japanese verse puzzle! He ran up the beach with the hot sand drying on his feet, scrambled into his green shirt and trousers and hurried into the marquee.

Michael Deane was there and gave the boy a friendly nod, and Colonel Chula waved him to a chair, but under the welcoming smile he studied the boy's face, noting the dark rings under the eyes from strain and lack of sleep, the hollow cheeks and the wary, instinctive glance around before he sat down. Yes, it was time to get him out.

'It is now the second day after your escape, Jason. Mr Deane and I both agree that the time has come for you to travel to Bangkok, where your father is waiting for you.' He held up his hand as Jason opened his mouth to speak. 'Please listen. I know – we both know – that you feel you cannot leave while those in the aircraft are still in danger, but negotiations are continuing. They may go on for days. And remember, if the hijackers hear of your presence and demand your return, we would be in a difficult position – and that journalist has photographed you here.'

Jason could think of nothing to say. Colonel Chula was right, of course: those hijackers would stick at nothing. It would be terrible if he only added to his difficulties. 'All right,' he muttered at last, 'I'll go.'

'Good.' Colonel Chula gave him a piercing glance. 'You continue to think of others.' He turned. 'Will you see Jason aboard the next helicopter, Mr Deane? I will arrange his reception and onward flight from Hat Yai, and Jason, my Government will see to an onward flight for you after you have had a chance to see your father.'

'Thanks,' said Jason in a low voice, looking down at the table.

'Remember, Jason – duty has the weight of a mountain.' It was Matsutan.

Jason looked up. The sympathy and understanding in the Japanese detective's face seemed to sharpen his sense of defeat. He heaved a deep sigh and blinked. That salt water still seemed to sting his eyes.

'Well,' said Deane briskly, getting up from his chair. 'We'd better see about this helicopter trip for you. At least you haven't any baggage to pack – no picnic hampers, like the rest of us!'

'I will accompany you to the helicopter,' said Matsutan formally.

'I must say goodbye here, Jason.' Colonel Chula held out his hand. 'I request, however, that when you pass through Bangkok on your next visit to your parents, you will break your journey and visit my home.'

They moved chatting to the marquee door when there was an interruption. Sumitomo appeared, face set in an expressionless mask but his eyes narrowed and glittering. He bowed to Colonel Chula, glanced round at the others, then handed Matsutan a slip of paper, bowed and straightened up again. He caught Jason's eye and gave him a quick slanting wink. Matsutan read it through

145

quickly, then said in English: 'The reply to our signal has arrived.' In dead silence he read out the Japanese phrases:

' "*Nigitazu ni,*
   Funanori sento," '

and looked up. 'Those were what we heard from Dar'a. According to this signal it is the first part of a *tanka* composed by the Princess Nukada some thirteen centuries ago, when a sea-borne expedition against Korea was about to sail. The remainder of this *tanka* goes:

"*Tsuki mateba,*
 Shio mo kanainu,
 Ima wa – kogi-ide na."

In English this means:

"The moon is full,
 The tide is high,
 Away! Let us put to sea!"

That part of the signal,' he said in his precise English, 'suggests that it applies to this situation exactly.'

'What other part is there?' asked Colonel Chula.

Matsutan looked down at the slip of paper in his hand. 'It is more a Japanese affair,' he said, but his voice held a note of triumph. 'A note explains that Nigitazu is the ancient name of the coastal town of Mitsugahama – in Iyo Prefecture.'

Jason looked up quickly.

'Well?' asked Colonel Chula.

'I suspected that the unknown leader in woman's dress might be a certain criminal – from Iyo!'

'Yasuno, of Iyo!' confirmed Sumitomo, unable to contain a smile of satisfaction.

'And the use of the classical *tanka*, not only as the signal for the success of the hijacking, the expedition, he would call it, but also containing a clue to his own identity – all that would appeal to a scholar.'

'Certainly, it all fits.' They were talking busily when there was another interruption. 'Tan!' A Thai orderly saluted and handed Colonel Chula a message form. He nodded dismissal to the orderly, moved the few paces back to his table and laid the message on it. Then he put both hands on the table and said in a reflective voice: 'There is a complication here which I had hoped would not arise.' He tapped the message which lay before him. 'This is from the meteorological centre in Bangkok – a storm warning for the Gulf of Siam. It will reach this area about midnight. Wind strengths will be Force Six, gusting to Force Eight, conditions will be severe and shipping is warned to stand out to sea.'

The listeners looked at each other, appalled. 'That aircraft will be driven right up on to the beach,' cried Deane. 'It'll break up!'

'I do not fear that so much,' said Matsutan. He looked at Colonel Chula, who nodded, and then at Deane. 'You have heard of Kamikaze, the Divine Wind of self-destruction in war?'

Deane gazed at him in horrified understanding. 'You don't mean – '

'I do mean that.' Matsutan's voice was again curt and grating. 'This storm they will take as their Divine Wind, as a sign. They are in a tense state. Wherever they look they see enemies. I fear that, rather than see the aircraft break open, their attempt ruined and themselves humiliated, they will blow themselves and the passengers to the skies.'

'Our Governments must be informed of this!'

'Mr Deane, they have been.' Colonel Chula spoke wearily. 'This signal is not addressed to me alone. What I *will* do is to give, most urgently, my opinion to my own Government, and Mr Matsutan – '

'My Minister here will understand.' Matsutan ran from the marquee.

'If Israel still does not budge – '

'Then Mr Deane, we may have to consider deception. But it is a great risk to take.'

'If we don't try it, the wreck of that aircraft will be up here among the palm trees by midnight, in darkness, or – '

'Or there may be no darkness left. Is that what you mean?'

'That may be the choice.'

Deane called, 'Jason! You'd better be off. Jason?' He looked about him. 'Where's that boy?' He walked quickly back to the tent. 'Jason!' he called, 'If you don't get a move on, you'll miss that helicopter! Can you hear me? Come on, Jason!'

Hidden by trees Jason listened unmoved. Only one thing mattered to him: tonight came the crunch. He was not going to leave till this was seen through. He could help, he didn't know why or how, but he knew he could help. He had never been so certain of anything in his life. Eventually Deane's calling stopped, but Jason still sat on. For an hour or two the air would crackle with messages, but the Governments would fail to agree. After that it would be up to the people on the beach.

He sat hidden among the trees for over an hour. The routine camp sounds had not altered and it seemed to him as if the significance of the storm warning had meant nothing. At last, when he felt it was safe to emerge, he left the trees and walked rather hesitantly through the palms to where Bill sat under the awning, and at sight of him the signaller's eyebrows rose. 'Hullo there! You're not very popular!'

'I'm sorry. I just couldn't go.'

'Well, I can't say I blame you – looks as if it's going to be settled one way or another by tonight. I'll make a brew.' He went over to the fire-blackened tin, shook up the sand in the bottom, poured in a half-cup of petrol and, standing well back, tossed in a match. The petrol-soaked sand whoofed, then burned steadily; he put on the kettle and sat back. 'Near enough tea-time anyway.'

'Where's Mr Deane?'

'He's in conference with that Thai police bloke – '

'Colonel Chula?'

'That's the one – and the Jap.'

'You heard about the storm?'

'Sure did. It's going to remove my aerial and our tents, if I know anything about these things.' He looked very thoughtful. 'Doesn't look too hopeful for the people in that aircraft – psychopathic hijackers on one side and a typhoon on the other.' He looked at Jason. 'You'd better have something to eat – I don't think you've had a proper meal since we saw you! When did you eat before that?'

'Well – I had supper on Sunday.'

'*Sunday*! It's Tuesday afternoon!'

'I had something last night.'

'Biscuits! We've got some bully here, and those Thais'll soon rustle something up. You'll be fit for nothing if you don't eat!'

'I don't want anything, thanks.'

Bill gave him a sharp look. 'Stomach all knotted up, eh? Is that how it feels?'

Jason nodded. The thought of food choked him.

'What you want is a good cup of sweet tea. It won't matter if you do without food for a day or two, never did anyone any harm. But tea, now – that'll make all the difference. Coming up.' He poured out a strong dark brew into a huge mug, added a heaped dessert-spoon of sugar, poured in unsweetened condensed milk till it grew creamy and stirred it. 'There you are,' he said, 'sergeant-major's tea. Get that lot inside you and you'll feel a new man.'

Whether it was his thirst and fatigue, or whether it was

the power of Bill's brew, but Jason felt he had never tasted such tea in his life. His tissues soaked up the sugary richness, and almost at once he felt relaxed and easier.

'Feeling better?'

'Much better.' Suddenly Jason ran with sweat, as if the hot tea was bursting straight out through his pores again.

'Yes, you look a bit cheerier. Ah, here's Michael.' Bill leant over to pour another mug. Jason got awkwardly to his feet, but Deane gave him a brief wave of the hand. 'Don't worry, Jason – no one'll force you to go.' He sank down into the chair and took the mug of tea with a silent nod.

'You're the one that looks worried,' said Bill. 'Anything doing?'

'Nothing.' He sipped at his tea. 'Frantic signals going out – and arguments coming back.'

'What sort of arguments?'

' – No deadline yet given, time still on our side, possibilities of demarche still open, all avenues being explored – the usual officialese.' He shook his head wearily. 'It's not realistic.'

'Here's the tape.' Bill held up the spool of clear plastic. 'I've got the Arabic, that Jap bit, and right on to the end of the programme.' He looked at Deane hopefully, 'I thought we might just need it.'

'It's the second half of that *tanka* we want,' Deane pointed out, 'not the first bit.'

'Easy! I'll get the detective to dub it in! And,' he added, 'it'll be in exactly the right spot, just where they're expecting to hear it. How about it. Can we give it a try?'

Slowly Deane shook his head. 'I really think it's too risky, and in any case, it's not our decision. The Thais are in charge, and they're running this thing far better than many other countries would. We mustn't attempt to influence their decisions in any way.'

Jason felt his impatience mount. That Japanese *tanka* was the key. With it his own flight in the forest, the death of the hijacker, the link with the Palestine Resistance, the *tanka* itself, about moon, tide and sea, and with its hidden reference to the disguised leader – all fitted and fell into place. If it were *not* the key, then everything became at once meaningless. He began to feel rather light-headed. Lack of sleep, two days without food, the sun's heat, his concentration on the fate of the prisoners in the aircraft – all made him feel remote, as if he were looking at the scene from a distance. He thought on to the dark of midnight, with the wind rising, the waves beginning to pound on the beach and the aircraft shifting, its under-carriage buckling as it was driven sideways – then light-ning flashes showing the hijackers up to their waists in water reaching up to the explosives, passengers beginning to jump out into the rising water, then the orange explo-sion, the fireball rising quickly, the shock wave, flaming oil pouring out over water and beach and people . . . He put down his mug and walked swiftly through between the tents.

The Thai sentry exclaimed, made a grab and missed and Jason ducked past him and ran into the marquee, and at the brief disturbance the group of men round the Minister at his desk looked up.

'You must try the tape, Sir,' said Jason without cere-mony, 'or the people in the plane will die.' He knew exactly what he had to say, and now that he had said it he did not resist when the sentry grabbed him and started to pull him away, but at a word from the Minister the sentry, still holding Jason, paused, and the officials converging on him stopped and moved back.

The Minister's placid, watchful eyes showed neither surprise nor anger at the unexpected interruption. 'I heard that you were to return to your parents today.' He paused a moment. 'It appears that you decided to stay.' He gave a barely perceptible shift of the eyebrows and the sentry saluted and returned to his post by the door.

'Yes, Sir.'

The Minister looked at the eyes which stared back into his own. The whites round the pale grey irises were very slightly bloodshot, either from lack of sleep, from the warm salt of the sea or from both, and the brown hair was edged with white, where sun had dried the sea-water. The eyes looked back at him calmly but with detachment as if a burden borne with great effort had finally been handed on.

'I have been informed about this tape,' said the Minister. 'If these men suspect they are being tricked, they may take the action we all fear.'

'When the wind and sea carry the plane up into the trees tonight, the people will die anyway.'

Unlike the bulky, smooth-faced Colonel Chula the Minister was a slight man, his bony face seamed with fine lines. He heard Jason's statement without comment, but his eyes never left Jason's face. At length he spoke. 'We are considering everything.' His tone, quiet and dispassionate, carried authority and conviction, and Jason sighed. It was no use, really; Bill's idea was too much of a technical trick. It was too flimsy. It could not deceive men who demanded a country's compliance but who secretly longed for a bloody, flaming holocaust. He thought back to Kimono's glare, and back farther to the anticipation in the face of the man who had reached out to throttle him in the little camp. In their minds was only death. 'I'm sorry,' he said, and turned away. He could do no more. Behind him the Minister spoke in Thai, and one of his staff hurried after Jason and caught him up outside. 'The Minister thanks you for your suggestion,' he said in formal

English, and Jason muttered something in reply. He began to feel hopeless: now that he was outside in the sunshine again, the hard glare throwing short shadows at his feet and the sea sparkling where it broke on the beach, the high outline of the aircraft's tail section visible over the marquee roof, he recognized what he had seen in the eyes of the men inside. It was weariness – not yet complete exhaustion, but the worn look of men who themselves had not slept for two nights, and who themselves bore a huge burden.

He looked at his watch: it was nearly three o'clock. Nothing seemed to be happening. Bill was preparing to make a call to the Embassy and Michael Deane and the Japanese were nowhere to be seen. Jason went into the empty tent and lay down on a blanket, looking up at the slack canvas above, the pattern of coarse weave outlined by the sun behind.

He knew now that he had played his last card. The key to the riddle, which he had in ignorance carried from the aircraft, for which he had been hunted and in turn had killed, and which Bill and Matsutan with their differing skills had identified, seemed to be too dangerous to use – as lethal as the explosive taped under the aircraft wing. It was no use thinking any more about it. The sense of defeat he had felt earlier returned, but this time it was complete. He was sick of this hot beach, of the long strain and worry. He began to wonder whether it was still too late to get a lift out in a helicopter. Then running feet crunched the sand, the tent flap was plucked open and the Thai office orderly peered in. 'Tan Deane?'

'Not here.' Jason looked up, shook his head and let it fall back again as the orderly ducked back out and hurried away, calling, 'Tan Deane! Tan Deane!'

There seemed to be a bit of movement going on, with urgent voices and running feet, but Jason lay without interest. The last forty-eight hours had been full of such sporadic hurry and bustle, and it had all made not a bit of difference: the fate of the passengers depended on remote men far away, and for one reason or another they were achieving nothing.

He did not know how long he had lain there when he heard the commotion of voices and hurrying feet back again. Once more the tent flap was plucked open, but this time it was Michael Deane's head that stuck in. 'Up you get, Jason!' His tone was peremptory, but his face wore a grim smile. 'Looks as if we're going to try Bill's idea.'

'The broadcast?' Jason stared up at him and then scrambled to his feet. 'We can try it?'

'If there's nothing else by five.' Deane hurried away towards the wireless awning and Jason ran after him.

Matsutan was already there, with Bill running the tape, and the others fell silent as they watched. 'Here we are.' Bill stopped the tape recorder, switched on to 'Play', they heard the rolling Arabic phrases, then came the blank crackle of static and the new voice, a deeper voice in different, curt tones. Bill ran the tape back in short bursts till it reached the point where the blank crackle of static began, switched off and looked up at Matsutan. 'Ready.'

'Play me the Japanese voice two or three times, please.'

He listened, nodding, his lips moving in time with the words, then saying along with them:

' "*Nigitazu ni,*
    Funanori sento – " '

At last he looked at Bill and slowly nodded. 'I will record the remainder.'

'I'll run the Arabic for a minute, then as soon as we hear the blank part before the Japanese, I'll stop. I'll switch it to "Record" and you must then begin, so that your voice will take over before there's a sound from the other fellow. All right?'

'*Hai!*' Matsutan ducked his head abruptly. 'I understand.'

'O.K.' Bill ran the tape back a moment, stopped it and switched to 'Play' and the Arabic phrases rolled out ... '*Sawt al-filistiniyah, Sawt ath-Thowrah al Filistiniyah* ...' The call-sign ended, the static crackled, Bill stopped the recorder, nodded to Matsutan and started it at 'Record'.

His voice deep and confident, pitched to exactly the tone and pace of that of the unknown terrorist, Matsutan spoke into the microphone:

' "*Tsuki mateba,*" ' he proclaimed,

' "*Shio mo kana-inu,*
   Ima wa – kogi-ide na!" '

Bill switched off. 'Right,' he said casually. 'Let's hear it. I'll start with a sentence or two in Arabic.' He ran it back and switched on to 'Play'. The Arabic sounded, the static-laden pause that followed was quickly broken by the voice of Matsutan and when it ended, Bill switched off again.

To Jason the voices appeared identical. 'Sounded all right to me,' said Bill. He laughed: 'A bit of static through that and it'd fool anyone!'

'Can you really dub in static?' Deane sounded doubtful.

'Something very like it!'

'But what's Mr Matsutan's own opinion?' Deane turned to him. 'You have said nothing.'

'It is my own voice.' Matsutan spoke in his old grating tones. 'We must ask someone else.' He looked across at Sumitomo.

'Will it do?' Deane asked him.

'Yes.' Sumitomo gave a short bow. 'It will do.'

'Now we wait.' Deane looked at his watch. 'It's well after three, and the Minister is giving his Government till five – and has told them so. Pity he waited so long to make his mind up – if he'd decided when he got the storm warning we'd have had that much more time.'

'Something made him see the light,' Bill grunted. 'Whatever it was, it was better late than never. Like all these blokes it's a question of the last minute. Hullo!' He looked beyond them. 'Here's the Colonel.'

He came walking between the tents towards them and glanced around in greeting.

'The two Ministers request a hearing of that tape. They are now taking this suggestion very seriously. They would like to discuss certain possibilities.'

'Of course.' Deane stood up. 'Bill, will you bring the tape? And Mr Matsutan – will you come?' The three of them set off for the headquarters marquee.

'I have a suggestion,' said Matsutan when the Ministers had heard the tape through. 'If this tape is to be used, it would be better if there were some confirmation from a different source that the demands were being met.'

'How is that possible?' The Thai Minister looked at him shrewdly. 'Anything from Thai sources would be suspected.'

'These men do not speak Thai,' said Matsutan. 'They listen, I suspect, to Tokyo radio's overseas broadcast for South Asia.'

'Even so – do you suggest that it be asked to transmit false news?' The Minister shook his head. 'It would never be allowed!'

'Not false news,' said Matsutan stiffly. 'Simply a statement that there is neither confirmation nor denial of new hopes that Israel will release the prisoners.'

'I understand what you mean.' The Thai Minister thought for a moment. 'That statement, of course, is quite true.'

'We may use it as a small seed to plant in their minds.'

All this while a rapid low-voiced translation had been going on for the benefit of the Japanese Minister, and when he had heard Matsutan's suggestion he questioned him briefly in Japanese, and after a moment's thought he nodded. 'Agreed.'

Under the awning Jason sat talking with Sumitomo. His lassitude had vanished, replaced by impatience. At last something seemed to be happening, and when Deane and the others returned he sprang up hopefully. 'Everything fixed?'

'Well, we had a long session.' Deane sank down. 'There's going to be a storm, all right – something's got to break.' He mopped his face and neck. 'Mr Matsutan here did most of the planning and I must say he did it very unobtrusively – made it all seem as if it was his chief's idea. Anyway, this is what we've worked out. The Minister is allowing up to four fifty-five for a move by outside Governments. If nothing happens by that time Bill will go ahead and prepare to transmit that tape, and will actually put it out at ten seconds to five. That is 1000 G M T, one of the times at which that station is transmitting.'

'So the deadline's at five?'

'That's it – but it's just the beginning.' Deane explained. 'Mr Matsutan is sure that they will want confirmation. One broadcast may be all very well, but these characters won't act on the strength of one broadcast. After all,' he gave a humourless smile, 'the announcer might have played the wrong recording!'

Bill grinned: 'That's been done before, and not a thousand miles from London, either!'

'So,' said Deane, 'they will want to make sure, and will listen to the next call.'

'But that'll be another two hours!' Jason felt his heart sink. A two-hour gap would bring them to seven in the

157

evening; he felt instinctively that it would be too late, and dangerous.

'Not so. We think that in the event of things happening in the right way they would start getting broadcasts *every hour*. That would also be a further confirmation. Get it?'

'So we'll try again at six!'

'Exactly. Then, with luck, we may get some results.'

'We'll have to watch them.'

Deane laughed. 'Jason, you should have been at the meeting, too! Yes, we're going to watch them, all right. Mr Matsutan and I'll watch from here, and the Thais of course have their observation post with everything – binoculars, film cameras, the lot. Any action to be taken is up to the Thais, of course; all we do is transmit, every hour. All right?'

'All right.'

Deane looked at his watch, then at Jason. 'You look nearly all in. I don't think you've been sleeping too well.'

('That,' thought Jason, 'is the understatement of the year!')

'If I promise to wake you five minutes before five, will you try and get an hour's kip?'

'Yes,' Jason blinked his eyes again. How they ached! 'Don't forget to wake me,' he said with an uneasy smile. He walked off clumsily, as if his movements were not quite co-ordinated. It was hot in the tent, the blanket warm as he lay on it. He closed his eyelids but the sun glowing through the tent canvas struck at the pricking eyes beneath. He groped around, felt the jungle hat beside him and pulled it over his face. One by one his muscles relaxed and he fell into a heavy sleep.

'No movement yet.' Michael Deane spoke without removing the binoculars from his eyes.

'It is only just four o'clock.' Flattened out in the sand beside him Matsutan turned up his wrist, looked at his watch and put his eyes back to his own binoculars. 'If they hear that Tokyo broadcast – which will be the main evening news in Japan – and it *does* give the item, it may not be first. It will have more effect if it comes as a news flash during the broadcast, as we requested.'

'That's cunning.' Deane swung the binoculars. 'No move from the men under the wing.' One, he saw, lay at full length, an arm behind his head in the sand, his Kalashnikov propped against his chest. The other, legs tucked beneath him, sat upright facing back, the passenger door on his left and the Thai sentries on his right. Deane looked at his watch again: three minutes past! He lowered his binoculars and lay gazing at the scene before him, now drearily familiar. Everything looked just as it had in the last thirty-six hours, the pattern apparently unchanged.

'Something!'

At Matsutan's exclamation Deane snatched up his binoculars again. 'Where?'

'Flight deck.'

The pale face appeared for a moment at the forward doorway. The third hijacker ran over and looked up. Deane focused on the doorway, but the pale-faced man kept well back. The man below stood listening, bowed slightly and walked back towards the others. They spoke for a moment, then the two under the wing resumed their positions, and the third man returned to his nook by the undercarriage.

'It may be nothing,' said Matsutan cautiously.

'Too much of a coincidence. Remember, they've got nothing else to do in there but listen. I think they heard Tokyo.'

'I also think so.' Matsutan rolled up his binocular strap

and put away the binoculars in their deep leather case. Together they walked back to the awning.

'Now we wait,' said Deane.

'Yes,' agreed Matsutan. 'It is like waiting for the battle.'

'Five to, Jason. Come on, now – time to get up!'

He turned his face this way and that, but there was no escape, and reluctantly he opened his eyes to see the tent canvas glowing and Deane's head framed against it. Mumbling he sat up, reaching about for his shoes while Deane tried to calm him: 'It's all right – nothing's happened yet, we're in good time –' and at last Jason remembered where he was and what was happening. He blinked and rubbed his eyes, still pricking with fatigue. 'We'll be putting out that tape in two or three minutes,' said Deane. 'The Minister's given us the go-ahead,' and Jason was up at once, and pulling on his shoes even while still not fully awake.

Seated around the awning was a small concourse of spectators. There was Colonel Chula, the Japanese Minister and the Thai Minister he had spoken to before, their orderlies behind them. Jason stopped. His green shirt and trousers were crumpled and baggy, striped black where he had sweated as he had lain asleep in the hot tent; his face must be flushed and his eyes red, and he knew that his hair had set in a lop-sided tangle. He felt like a tropical tramp, but Deane took him firmly by the elbow and steered him to a spot on the sand where they could both see Bill sitting with his eyes on the watch in front of him.

'Fifty seconds to go,' he said.

No one stirred. Jason kept his eyes on the sand, unwilling to risk distracting Bill by giving him so much as a look.

'Twenty seconds.'

In the silence Jason heard the faint slap and rustle of the incoming tide.

'Five seconds . . . three, two, one – ' and Bill flicked the switch to 'Transmit'.

11

WAVES

'THEY should get the bait' – Deane looked at his watch – 'in six minutes.'

But would they take it? Jason sat listening to the faint, almost imperceptible hiss of the tape being played silently into the transmitter. Occasionally Bill made a fractional adjustment of the volume control, keeping the needle steady. Deane nudged Jason and whispered: 'We'll go and watch them.'

Matsutan already lay on the sand ridge with his binoculars trained on the aircraft, and they stretched out near him.

'Here, Jason,' murmured Deane. 'You started all this!'

Jason took the old binoculars and focused them on the figures of the hijackers under the wing, sprawled out and apparently oblivious to whatever the wireless set in the cabin announced. 'What's the time?' he asked Deane, whispering to avoid disturbing Matsutan.

'Four minutes past.'

'Those chaps are just lying there.'

'They've heard a dozen of these Arabic broadcasts in the last two days. They don't know this one's going to be any different – yet.'

'But they heard that Tokyo one!'

'It didn't really say anything – it should just make them accept the other more easily. One more minute.'

Jason put the binoculars down and closed his eyes to rest them. He wanted them to be sharp and clear when he looked again. Cautiously he drew a sleeve across his forehead to dry off the trickle of perspiration, with all the while his mind ticking off the seconds. When he estimated that forty seconds had passed he opened his eyes and lifted the binoculars again, then counted to twenty. They must be hearing it! Surely that pale-faced terrorist would at this very moment be staring at the wireless set and listening to what he wanted to hear.

'*Ai! Miro!*'

'There he goes!'

The two exclamations burst out simultaneously. The watchers saw a movement at the forward door. The third hijacker began walking towards it, broke into a run, paused to listen, then turned back and called something to the men under the wing, and they jumped to their feet.

'They've heard it!'

Yes, they had heard it, thought Jason – but would they

believe it? He could not see the pale-faced man, so he turned his binoculars on the men under the wing. They were standing and by their movements he knew they were talking rapidly to the third man, who glanced frequently back up towards the cabin.

For the first time Matsutan lowered his binoculars and acknowledged the presence of the others. He let out his breath in a long sigh. 'I think they have believed it.'

'How can you tell?' Deane asked.

'See how they stand eagerly talking? Never once have they looked back towards the Thai sentries or at all those people who watch them.'

'Well?'

'They think what they discuss concerns only themselves and the fida'i far away. If they thought that the Thais had any hand in this broadcast they would turn and face them, looking to see who was watching for their reactions.'

'Of course!'

Jason smiled at the surprise in the other man's voice. Deane was just beginning to discover what Jason already knew – that beneath his impassive exterior Matsutan was a very sharp observer of human behaviour.

'Number three – isn't that Hara? – is off again!' Both pairs of binoculars swung up. 'He's going up the ladder – he's taken something!' They watched as he climbed down again and followed him as he walked towards the enclosure rope. 'He's giving something to the sentry!' Jason saw the hijacker hand the Thai soldier something small and white. 'It's a piece of paper.'

Matsutan wriggled backwards, and once out of sight of the aircraft hurried round to the headquarters marquee. The message was delivered by the sentry at a run and quickly translated by the Japanese interpreter. 'This says that naval vessels should stand off from the aircraft.'

'Nothing else?' asked the Thai Minister. 'No explanation?'

'Nothing, Sir.'

'Very well.' He turned to Matsutan. 'You have studied these men. Is it possible that they will wait till morning?'

'If they do, the storm will decide for them. But these men will want to slip away in darkness. They will want to gain the advantage of a full night's travel. It may make the difference to them of escape or destruction at sea.' Matsutan nodded. 'If they believe the broadcasts, they will go when it is dark. But,' he hesitated, 'there is one more thing.' He paused.

'What is that?' asked the Thai Minister.

'I fear that they may take hostages with them till they are safely out of reach. It is a common terrorist practice.'

'There is nothing we can do.' The Minister spoke decisively. 'We must think of the majority.'

Matsutan shrugged and bowed all at the same time, but the lines on his face deepened as he walked slowly back.

At the rattle of winch and anchor chain Deane swung his binoculars. 'Hullo – *Chanthara's* getting steam up!'

'Yes, Mr Deane – that was all that there was in that message from the hijackers. I think it is enough. They will go tonight.'

'But that's wonderful news!' Deane looked hard at the Japanese detective. 'You look worried. Do you think something will go wrong?'

'I do not think that anything will go wrong. I think they will leave in darkness. But I warned the Minister that they may take hostages with them.'

'What did he say?'

'He said that we must think of the majority.'

'I'm very much afraid he is right,' said Deane gently. 'But it is possible that they may *not* take hostages. In the event we can do nothing that would not risk the lives of everyone.'

'You are, of course, correct.' Matsutan bowed stiffly. 'The matter is out of our hands.'

'Again, we must wait.'

'That's *that* lot!' Bill sat back from the set. 'End of broadcast – nothing now for another forty minutes. Time for tea!' He wiped his face and winked at Jason. 'A *proper* cup of tea!'

'The tide's coming in – how about a swim while Bill's brewing up?' suggested Deane. 'It'd pass the time and help us cool off.'

'Good idea.' Jason stripped and they ran down to the water.

'At least this is better than a hot airport!' Deane called cheerfully as he splashed about clumsily in the shallows. Jason waved and slipped into the water, and with a flick of wrist and foot shot along the sandy bottom, then rising without a ripple and turning to float on the surface. At a splash near him he opened his eyes in quick alarm, but relaxed as he saw Matsutan swimming out towards him.

For some moments they lay drifting in companionable silence till Matsutan said: 'Jason, there is a problem.'

'Yes?' Jason lay lazily floating. He assumed that the Japanese detective had discovered some technical difficulty to do with the hijackers, but what it was he couldn't imagine. Surely things were going even better than they had dared hope!

'Jason, we think that they will certainly take hostages with them in the boat.'

'To get them past the gunboats?'

'*Hai.*' Matsutan stopped floating and stood up in the waist-deep water. 'They are going in a big launch, but there are now only four of them, not five as they had expected. If they head out to sea, they will all four be

166

busy. They will not want big troublesome hostages who will be difficult to control.'

Jason tried to shut his mind to what Matsutan was saying, but the detective went on remorselessly: 'Who are weak and easy to control, Jason? Who will also cause the greatest outcry and recrimination from the world?'

Crouched in the water, his chin just above the surface, Jason felt rather sick.

'Surely the children. And Jason, what will happen to them when the hijackers find they have been tricked?'

Jason stood up and started to wade towards the shore. Matsutan was right. Ever since he had mentioned hostages, Jason had known that the children would be taken, but he had refused to let himself think of it. He reached the sand and sank down on to it. The sense of hopelessness that had borne so heavily on him till only a short while ago returned, now heavier than ever. Whatever he did seemed only to make things worse. He had escaped, and that Japanese hijacker had died. Because he had died, the hijackers were one man short and would choose the children as hostages. He had remembered the key word, Arabic, and all the deception that had sprung from that might well result only in yet more deaths.

Matsutan sat down beside him. 'Jason – Sumitomo and I are going to rescue those children.'

Jason did not reply. He did not take Matsutan seriously till the detective said: 'We ask for your help.'

'Mine? But we mustn't try anything like that! They would set off the explosive!'

'That should not happen.' Matsutan spoke with curt assurance. 'Listen, please. We know they will leave by sea, and we are sure that they will go in darkness. For one thing, that leader will want to leave unidentified.'

'Yes, that is so.' Jason listened without much conviction.

167

'It is dark by seven, and moonrise tonight is at seven thirteen precisely. I consider that they will try to leave between those two times.'

'Yes, probably.'

'Sumitomo and I will try to take the children from the boat after the hijackers leave the aircraft, so the passengers will be safe. But we cannot get the children away without your help.'

Jason sat hugging his knees. He sensed a terrible choice opening before him: either a refusal to help, with a consequent lifelong burden of doubt and shame if the children were killed, or involvement in some suicidal rescue attempt.

'We do not want you to fight these men,' said Matsutan calmly. 'We only want you to help take the children away in the water.'

Jason looked round at him. 'It doesn't matter. I will help.' He didn't know quite why he spoke or what had prompted him to agree. He felt slightly worse after he had said it, as though he had agreed to his own extinction.

Matsutan nodded as if that was the answer he had expected. 'I ask you for several reasons,' he said. 'We are Japanese, and the children will not recognize us as friends. I remember that you told me how you used to read to the children. They know your name – and they will remember your voice. Finally, of the English here, only you swim well.'

'Does Mr Deane know about this?'

'No. He would forbid you to go. He would ask to come himself, but,' Matsutan shook his head, 'he would be noisy and clumsy in the water. We must be silent, like the fish in the sea.'

'And the Thais?'

'They would forbid it outright, in case it endangered the others. But it will not.' Matsutan spoke with certainty.

'Just how will we do it?'

'Let us first think what the hijackers will do. I think that they will send the engineer, Hara, to start up the diesels as soon as it is dark. Then, when they are running properly, two men will carry the children out and hand them into the boat and climb in themselves. Finally the last man, who has been covering the rear, will climb aboard and they will head out along the coast, in shallow water – too shallow for the gunboats, who in any case will not open fire because of the children. That,' said Matsutan, 'is how I think they will plan.'

Jason sat thinking. That sounded absolutely right – and impossible to prevent. He knew in his bones that it was exactly what the hijackers were planning. 'How can we stop them without' – he hesitated, groping for a word – 'harming the children?'

'We will swim round from the rocks. As soon as the engineer has started the diesels, we will silence him, and I will take his place.'

'The others'll spot you at once!'

'I do not think so. Remember,' said Matsutan with a faint smile, 'I speak Japanese. Also, it will be very dark, the diesels will be running and they will be in a hurry.'

'And the children?'

'I will pass them over the side and you and Sumitomo will swim away with them.'

'But what about you?'

'I will hold off the three hijackers. No,' he held up a hand, 'do not protest. I will have the advantage. Do not forget that I will be in the boat and they in the water.'

'H'm.' Jason was very doubtful. In theory it sounded fine – but one bitter lesson he had learnt in the last forty-eight hours was how widely divergent theory and practice could be. The plan seemed feasible enough, but something about it disturbed him. He could visualize himself swimming away – if necessary with both children, towing them backstroke – and he could visualize Matsutan holding off the others. What he could *not* see was Matsutan climbing aboard without alerting the engineer – and one burst from his Kalashnikov would tell the other three hijackers, still near the aircraft, that their means of escape was being boarded. Jason felt cold. Not only would the attempt fail, but some maniac like Kimono would blow up the aircraft while the passengers were spilling out of it.

'That engineer will shoot you,' he said gruffly, rude in his anxiety. 'He's bound to have his gun with him.' Looking away in his awkward distress Jason did not see the faint gleam of amusement in the slanting brown eyes. 'He must see me first,' said Matsutan, 'and even then he will have to be quick.' He looked out to sea. 'The clouds approach, and already it grows cooler.'

Jason felt a touch of goose-flesh prickle his skin, but whether from the first faint breeze of the coming storm or his own foreboding he could not tell.

'We will meet at the rocks just before seven, when it is nearly dark. You will be there and ready, Jason?'

'Yes. I will be there.'

'Soon be dark.' Deane peered at his watch. 'Bill's going to transmit again at seven.'

Jason fidgeted. Lights were springing up in the tents behind them, but the beach was still pale against the sea. Crossing it unnoticed to join the two Japanese was an unexpected problem, as was avoiding arousing Deane's curiosity.

'I'm going round to the front,' said Deane. 'It'll be safe enough for you in the dark. Coming?'

'Yes, sure.' Jason thought swiftly. 'I'll follow you round – I'll just go down and wash off some of this sand.' He set off with his towel at a casual walk and half-way down the beach looked back. The single lamps shone in each tent; a little way out from them Bill's face, intent, was illuminated by the tiny light over the dials of his set, and behind him palms and forest and ridge merged into a black background. There was no sign of Deane's tall figure and Jason broke into a run.

'Jason?' There was a hint of impatience in Matsutan's voice. 'We must not delay.' The two men were hidden among the rocks, and Jason slipped off his rubber shoes and began to undress.

'Do not undress.' The whisper floated to him. 'You will shine in the water.'

Jason nodded at this very practical piece of advice. Keeping on his crumpled olive-green shirt and trousers would make swimming a trifle less slick, but it would make him, apart from his white feet, indistinguishable in the water, and he blessed the sun of the open beach which had darkened his face. The two Japanese, he now made out, also wore dark clothing, the grey worsted trousers of their suits, and over their bare chests and arms the neat knitted jerseys that had helped to keep out the bitter winds of a Tokyo winter only three days ago. Jason had a quick vision of what his mother would say were he to go swimming in his best suit, and choked back a nervous laugh.

'It is two hundred yards from here,' whispered Matsutan, 'but we must swim out and approach it from the sea. It will be nearly three hundred that way.'

Jason hesitated. Everything was quiet. There was still no activity from the aircraft. Surely by now there would have been some indication that a move was afoot, a light flashing about; some movement? Matsutan sensed his unease. 'If we are wrong, we will just swim quietly back and wait.'

'But when they take the children – '

'The last man will hold the others quiet at gun-point. Now, let us go.'

A skirr of rain roughened the surface of the sea and was gone, and a distant lightning flash lit up the heart of a cloud, leaving the darkness intense. 'They will think that Heaven supports them,' the detective murmured, half to himself, 'but Heaven is working for us.' He looked round at his two younger companions and between his teeth hissed: 'Jason, Sumitomo – *banzai*!'

They sank into the water and swam out noiselessly from the rocks. They swam fast and silently, using the breast-stroke. Jason could just make out Matsutan's head in front of him, rising and dipping, with Sumitomo a little to his right. In a few moments they were round the end of the promontory and Jason caught a glimpse of the patrol boat. Rain still spotted the surface of the water but in addition the faint breeze had freshened and small waves had sprung up. The patrol boat had swung as the tide turned, and now lay at the end of her taut hawser, bows pointing inshore and the twin screws of the stern facing back out to sea. Some eighty yards beyond rose the dark hump of the aircraft, blotting out a segment of the light pattern on shore.

They swam in a half-circle, approaching the patrol boat from the sea. When they were within fifty yards of her they slowed down and, swimming just enough to make way, closed in. At a hiss from Matsutan they stopped and waited, treading water. There was a slight swell, and the dark shape of the patrol boat, now only twenty yards away, rose and fell. As on the night before small cooking fires blazed on the sand, and their sparks floated up and died among the palm fronds. A snatch of music – possibly from the same Thai orchestra – floated across the water to them from some soldier's radio, interspersed by snatches of talk. It was so normal, thought Jason – so peaceful. Perhaps the hijackers weren't going to make their attempt at all!

The patrol boat seemed to be dipping a trifle more to one side, and Jason wiped the water from his face and eyebrows as he strained to see better. There was a small splash, a bump-scrape, the slap of wet feet on deck planking and a stocky figure was outlined briefly against the lights of the shore. He vanished into the shadows, there was silence again, then the self-starter whined, the diesels burst into life, raced a moment and settled down into a steady, noisy chug, and smoke bubbled back from the stern exhausts.

Matsutan tapped Jason's shoulder and whispered into his ear: 'Stay back.' In half a dozen quick strokes, the two Japanese reached the boat. Treading water, eyes and nose just above the surface, Jason watched from the darkness, half-deafened by the chug of engines.

In the cockpit below the wheelhouse a tiny light glowed on the figure of Hara the engineer, dimly outlined as he stooped, head cocked, listening to the throb of the diesels. Then Matsutan, his foot on Sumitomo's shoulder, slithered up and over the after gunwale and crouched behind the pair of oil drums lashed on deck. Hara raced the engines once or twice, and, satisfied, switched off and let them cough into silence. He put out the small light, climbed up on to the deck and with a pencil torch flashed a signal towards the aircraft. From the forward cabin came an answering flash and, as Hara bent to put the torch away, Matsutan stepped silently out from behind the oil drums and struck him hard just below the junction of jaw and ear.

From the dark water Jason saw only the silent movement, like shadow play: the stocky hijacker, the equally stocky Matsutan moving behind him, the two outlines merging – and then one lifting the other down into the wheelhouse and folding it away out of sight.

Jason swam quickly to the hull, and with Sumitomo clung to the stern. Still there was no disturbance on the shore – but Sumitomo moved his head, and Jason knew he had seen something. He let himself float out from the hull and looked past him along the surface. At first he could make out nothing against the dark background of the aircraft, then from the cloud came a lightning flash and momentarily illuminated he saw two men wading out towards the boat, one a dozen yards behind the other, each carrying something slung roughly over one shoulder and held by one arm, the other holding an automatic up out of the water. They were moving towards the patrol boat as quickly as they could wade.

12
DIVINE WIND

As the two hijackers left the high shadow of the aircraft, Jason saw their outlines clearly against the glow from the beach. The leading man, now with water rippling to his chest, and moving more slowly, called forward in a low voice. Matsutan, cupping his hands round his mouth, replied, and the hijacker came on steadily, half-wading and half-swimming, till he was close enough for Jason to hear the water swirl away behind him.

Passing below the high bows he pushed himself along till he was amidships, hoisted his silent burden up into the boat, laid his automatic on the deck planking with a slight clatter and heaved himself up out of the water and over the gunwales. Barely breathing Jason heard the slap of wet feet on the planking, a low voice and a muttered reply. Footsteps moved aft from the wheelhouse, someone spoke again, his voice became a coughing gasp, it was cut off abruptly, and the sound of low thumps was lost in the ripple and splash of waves against the hull.

Whether from strain or fear or simply from the night chill Jason began to shake and shiver in the water. His teeth chattered, he clamped his jaws tight together, yet still his cheek and jaw muscles twitched. He put his knuckles into his mouth to stop the faint noise – then suddenly he was alert again. The second man was bumping along round the hull and Jason shrank further down into the water. Though vague and shadowy he knew that shape. It was Kimono. He too dumped his burden, but he did not climb aboard. With a grunted word to the dark figure by the wheelhouse he turned and, half-swimming, half-wading, made off back towards the aircraft. Jason caught his breath: this was a development they had not expected – then he looked round. The moon was rising behind them, glimmering fitfully through low, heavy clouds.

'Jason! Sumitomo!' the boat rocked slightly as Matsutan carried the children towards the stern and Jason held up his arms as a child was lowered down to him. He allowed himself one glance: long fair hair plastered the white face and the small light body lay limp and unmoving in the crook of his arm – then he set both feet against the hull and pushed himself away. Near him Sumitomo had already set off, and they swam beside each other with desperate surges of effort, straining to move through the water yet avoid breaking the surface and alerting the hijackers with an incautious splash. Lightning flickered along the horizon. It lit up Matsutan's head and shoulders by the wheelhouse and then all was dark once more, but the rumble of thunder was longer and louder, and dark clouds covered the moon. For some moments they swam on in darkness and Jason began to hope that they might reach the rocks undetected – and then a longer, brighter series of lightning flashes flared out.

It was rather as if weak lighting had been switched on for a second over a vast watery stage. Behind stretched the curve of beach with its backdrop of palms and forest and in front the huge aircraft; eighty yards out, the patrol boat, long and grey, rode at the end of its hawser, and half-way between Kimono stood in the water, his automatic up, ready to cover the escape of the last man. The lightning died, but Jason heard the faint splash from the nose wheel as he swung down from the forward door, and dropped into the water. It was the leader, Yasuno – in the beach glow Jason saw the white and bloodless face – and he too held up an automatic as he waded out to sea.

For a moment the quiet persisted, then several things happened at once. A woman screamed and Jason heard ' – Children!', a light clicked on, illuminating the aircraft from one side, half-a-dozen Thai soldiers sprinted down, set bamboo ladders up to the wing root and began defusing the explosives still taped to the wing; someone roared 'Out – everyone out!' and from the after door people jumped down into the water or scrambled down the ladder. The canvas escape-chute billowed out, from the starboard hatches people poured out on to the wing and slipped or jumped down in the waist-deep water, tripping and splashing as they waded furiously for the beach and safety, while police and soldiers ran into the water to help them away. Last of all went the crew.

The glow from the new light on the beach lit up the aircraft and the sea immediately below it, but there was no attempt to floodlight the escaping hijackers, and Jason knew that the grim message about the children had been understood. He glanced back and saw Yasuno still wading on, outlined against the lights. Swimming on his back with the small burden occupying one arm was slow and clumsy work, and Jason tried to focus his mind on reaching the safety of the rocks, but he could not resist twisting his head to look. Still Yasuno came on, apparently unnoticing, and Jason's heart bounded as Matsutan switched on the diesels again and the steady beat of the engines throbbed out. That might well hold their attention and keep them from looking in the direction of the swimmers! Just a few more minutes, that was all he asked!

Lightning flashed, very close, and was followed at once by a heavy clap of thunder, then a cold wind whipped up the waves and spray broke from the tops. For a few seconds all was dark again, then lightning flared and flickered across the sea behind them, the dazzling flashes lighting up the swimmers in the water, and Yasuno, still some yards short of Kimono, stopped and flung out an arm. Kimono jerked round, stared, and his head thrust forward as if he could not believe what he saw – then he snapped his automatic up to his shoulder and squinted along the sights.

'They've seen us!' Jason's shout cut through the throb of the diesels. Beyond him Sumitomo vanished in a swirl of water, and as he took a last hasty gulp of air Jason saw the shocking sight of a muzzle flaming out towards him and heard the quick tearing 'brrrp' of a burst of automatic fire.

With a wriggle of his legs and a pull of his cupped hand he twisted himself down below the surface and turned to his right, towards the sea, but he was hampered by the child in his grasp and blundered under water into Sumitomo, who had gone straight on. They floated gasping to the surface in a tangle of arms and legs, and struck out desperately for the rocks again. He must dive – but he himself was coughing water and from the body in his arms there was no movement. If he dived again the child – perhaps already dead – would not survive. He struck out openly on the surface, careless of the tell-tale splashes, again he heard automatic fire and then the diesels roared up and he twisted his head again to look.

Chest-deep in the water, automatics to their shoulders, Kimono and Yasuno were firing in short rapid bursts, and bearing down on them in a swirl of bow wave and foaming wake was the patrol boat, Matsutan dimly visible through the wheelhouse glass. Still grasping his automatic, Kimono floundered to his left, but Matsutan swung the wheel and the bows struck the hijacker and ploughed on over him in the water. The boat swung back towards Yasuno, the diesel roar and the short frantic bursts of automatic fire all mixed up, then it reached the end of the hawser and jerked round. Jason lost sight of Yasuno in the swirling water, the boat swung again, engines roaring wildly; it set out seawards, reached the end of the hawser cable and this time jerked the anchor clean away from its grip on the sandy bottom. Dragging it and bearing sideways the boat swung towards the rocks, out of control and Matsutan no longer visible.

'Sumitomo!' Jason shouted and thrashed through the water away from the path of the roaring patrol boat. It careered past him, gathering speed, raced rocking from side to side over the choppy sea and seemed to fling itself on the rocks of the promontory. The engines hissed and steamed as sea-water rushed in, then spluttered, faltered and died.

Swimming openly on the surface Jason and Sumitomo reached the rocks, pulled themselves up and hurriedly carried the children to the first patch of sand. 'Quick – massage, respiration!' They worked with barely a glance at the shore, now ablaze with light and swarming with people. All attention seemed to be focused on the passengers streaming away from the aircraft, now beginning to shift sideways under the growing pressure of the rising wind and the scouring action of the waves on the sand under the great wheels, but one group of Thai soldiers, led by a bulky figure in plain clothes, ran into the darkness towards the promontory and began to scramble across the rocks just as the heavens opened and rain swept in from the sea.

Drenched at once, and shouting to make himself heard above the wind and rain, Colonel Chula directed his men to carry back the children – now beginning to stir and cry a little – and to drag out the three men in the wreck of the patrol boat.

The two hijackers were still unconscious, but Matsutan's

eyes were open, and he gasped apologies as he was lifted out: 'Regret no time to slip hawser – the children?'

'Both safe.'

'Don't talk.' Jason was frantic with worry. Matsutan's head and chest had been gashed by flying glass, and blood mixed with rain was soaking through his jersey and trousers. By comparison the single bullet wound in the right upper arm, which had knocked him away from the wheel as the boat jerked round, looked almost negligible, but the arm itself was broken and hung at his side. Screaming wind and rain now battered down at them, and water streamed down their faces as they struggled over the wet rocks.

On the beach was confusion, with lights flickering out and tents collapsing in a welter of wet canvas and dragging guy-ropes. The two doctors and the orderlies were busy lashing a rough windbreak shelter just inside the tree-line, and as he stumbled up the beach with Sumitomo and Matsutan, the way lit by the occasional terrifying glare of lightning flashes, Jason saw a woman in steward-ess's uniform helping to carry away the two children – safe at last.

They hurried the wounded detective up to the make-shift medical shelter where, by the light of a battery-oper-ated emergency lighting system, the doctors bound up his wounds and set his arm in temporary splints. Finally he was lifted down and left to rest on a stretcher protected from the worst of the wind by a shelter of flysheet held down by boxes of stores and equipment, and Sumitomo and Jason huddled down beside him to wait out the dark-ness and the storm.

Morning dawned soft and fresh, the green rags of the palm fronds motionless against the clean washed blue of the sky. The storm had blown itself out hours before, but the rising sun shone on a scene of indescribable confusion. The beach itself had been scoured clean by the pounding waves, and the sand was white and smooth again, as if no foot had been set on it. But the palm line and the first fringe of forest beyond were a tangle of tent canvas, bedding, equipment of all sorts, wires and cable and snapped and broken branches. Most grotesque of all, among the palms sat Speedwing II, its huge tail plane nudging a clump of coconuts and one wing caught between two forest trees.

Bleary-eyed passengers sat in the trampled lallang. Kept awake much of the night by the roaring of the storm, the lashing rain and the cold, they were physically worn out but in high spirits. Now they looked up at the calm sky and many fell asleep in the warming sunshine.

Gradually threads of smoke arose from cooking fires. Colonel Chula set his men to organizing tea and breakfast, but wisely left the sleepers alone. *Chanthara* steamed in close and began transmitting to the world the news that all were safe and the Thai Minister held an impromptu press conference, but refused to give details of the rescue of the children on security grounds.

The doctors waited for the morning's crop of injured from the night of falling trees and flying branches, but the move to the open lallang had forestalled damage, and they were left with Matsutan as their only serious casualty, and he was rescued from beneath the soaking flysheet and installed in considerable style under an awning beneath the palms.

Jason and Sumitomo watched sleepily and, once Matsutan was carried away, they looked at each other and laughed, but without much humour. The clothes they had swum in were crumpled and baggy and stained, and Jason spoke with concern: 'Those are your own clothes – your private clothes.' His own green shirt and trousers had been a gift from the Thais and could be washed, but the Japanese detective's trousers, shrunken and ruined by salt water, were probably his best office suit – chosen to look smart in when he hurriedly left Tokyo. Sumitomo bowed slightly: 'It is possible that my department may arrange reimbursement.'

'I should jolly well think so!' said Jason indignantly. 'Come on, let's look for some breakfast.' For the first time for days he was ravenous.

But as they walked quickly through the scattered groups drying themselves out they were intercepted. A worried-looking orderly saluted and indicated they should follow, waving to them to run.

'Now for Colonel Chula,' said Jason uneasily to the Japanese. He tried to sound cheerful but felt only apprehensive.

Seated on a rescued camp chair among the wreckage, with soldiers spreading out the soaking canvas of the marquee on the beach, Colonel Chula looked just as sleepy and thoughtful as ever. To Jason's surprise, however, he did not show anger; instead, he told them pleasantly that Matsutan's wounds were not grave. 'The doctor classified them as "moderate",' he said with a smile, 'though they look bad. We will fly him to hospital later today. Now – perhaps you will tell me just what went on last night?'

Jason automatically looked at Sumitomo, and found the young detective looking at him. 'Please,' he said, 'you speak English.' So Jason explained while Colonel Chula listened without interrupting. 'At least it worked,' he said when Jason had finished, 'but for your own security' – and his eyes bored into Jason's – 'you must not be known to have had anything to do with this. Do you understand me?'

'Yes, I understand.' Jason nodded. Colonel Chula looked past him. A Thai soldier, saluting stiffly, spoke and pointed back, and Colonel Chula stood up. 'Come, please,' he said, and Jason and Sumitomo followed him as he walked quickly along the beach and turned into the tangle of forest where a soldier stood waiting. A few feet in, the doctor knelt examining a body caught among twigs and seaweed and branches. Jason took one look and looked away.

'Skull fracture,' said the doctor, 'but the other injuries could also have been the cause of death.'

'So I see,' said Colonel Chula dryly. 'What happened to him?' He turned to Jason and Sumitomo. 'That is why I brought you both here. Do you know how this man died, Jason?'

'Yes.' The picture was sharp and clear. 'It was the patrol boat. It hit him, then went over him.'

'Ah, yes – that explains these other injuries. The propellers struck him.'

Jason stole another look. The Thai police were searching the dead man's pockets, but they held only wet sand.

'We'll be able to get his fingerprints,' commented Colonel Chula, 'but it's not much use taking a photograph. Even his mother would not know him now.'

'I know who it is.' Jason spoke clumsily, the memory of his fear returning. 'It is the man I called Kimono.'

'That is one Kashigawa,' explained Sumitomo.

'Are you sure?' asked Colonel Chula. 'How do you know it is not the leader?'

'This man was nearest. I saw the boat hit him.'

'Did you see what happened to the other?'

'I lost sight of him in the propeller wash when the boat turned.'

'H'm.' Colonel Chula took a long breath. 'Perhaps he was struck and killed or was drowned. If so, he too will be washed ashore. We will know in a few minutes. I have had the search extended. As for you two, I am going to send you to your Embassies in Bangkok before the press can get hold of you. They are too busy drying out their belongings and interviewing passengers to worry about things they know nothing about. I am also sending out Mr. Deane and your friend Bill. You will all travel in the first helicopter. And this time,' he bent a mock-fierce glance at Jason, 'you will please leave!'

'Yes, Sir.' Jason smiled. 'And Mr Matsutan?'

'Special arrangements. He will go out with one of the doctors as a malaria patient.' Colonel Chula drew on his cheroot. 'He will not be troubled. Now, please prepare to leave on the first helicopter.'

They walked briskly back and at the edge of the lallang found Deane and Bill, the giant picnic hamper between them, and Bill's case of wireless equipment. 'You've been busy!' Bill winked. 'What did you do to get us all turned out?'

'Breakfast, Jason – and Mr Sumitomo. Come along, we've got a few minutes before our helicopter's expected!' Deane opened the hamper. 'No bacon and eggs, I'm afraid – only packaged stuff!'

But Jason's eyes gleamed. There were biscuits and rye-bread and marmalade and tinned butter and triangles of cheese and tins of sardines – on which Sumitomo's eyes fastened – and while they were laying out all this, Colonel Chula's orderly came up with a beaming smile on his face and a tray in his hands, and set it before them with a flourish.

'My,' said Deane with feeling, as steam rose from the dishes, 'Siamese rice, curried eggs, chicken – ' he delved into the hamper for large plates. 'We must eat this while it's hot.'

While the breakfast party were busily absorbed, Colonel Chula was looking towards a solitary figure walking slowly along the beach from the south, a short figure in dishevelled clothing, slung about with the discoloured and water-stained cases of camera and tape recorder, and with thinning fair hair pushed back in a tangle. Colonel Chula sent a soldier to fetch him, and when he arrived looked in silence at the exhausted man before speaking. 'Good morning, Mr Bedford. You chose a bad time to travel.'

The journalist did not reply, and shook his head at Colonel Chula's offer of a cheroot.

'No? Please excuse me if I smoke.' The Colonel selected one, lit it carefully and put the case back in his pocket. 'Now, Mr Bedford, what have you done with your boatman?'

'He's repairing his mainmast. He's quite safe.'

'I am glad to hear it. How far did you travel before the storm came up?'

'I don't know. All I know is that before we realized it, we were blown on to the beach.'

'Well, then – how long have you been walking?'

'Since the storm died down.'

'H'm – that is some four or five hours. That means,' he cocked an eye at Bedford and at the sand, 'perhaps two miles an hour on this – you have walked some ten miles, no more.'

'It feels like a hundred,' said the journalist bitterly. His eye roamed over the beach, the trampled lallang and the astonishing sight of Speedwing II perched among the palms, and scowled.

'I fear that you missed the events of the evening,' said the Thai Colonel solicitously, 'but no doubt your many friends among the rest of the press corps will be glad to share their experiences with you, and probably let you have copies of their photographs.'

Bedford made no reply, but his scowl deepened.

'By the way,' Colonel Chula's tone changed from silk to steel. 'Those photographs you took of the boy and the

Japanese detective – give me them, please.' He held out his hand and reluctantly the journalist fumbled in his pocket and took out a sealed aluminium tube. 'Thank you, Mr Bedford – you may go now, but remember, if you ever think of coming to our country again, you would be wise to make no mention of what is in this film. Is that understood?'

The journalist hesitated, looked at the film in Colonel Chula's hand, then finally nodded. 'Agreed.'

Their empty plates rinsed clean with sand and sea-water and the dishes returned, the breakfast party were packing the hamper when they heard the racket of the morning's first helicopter low over the ridge. Colonel Chula hurried along towards them. 'Nearly time to go, Gentlemen. My soldiers will help with your things.'

'I must see Matsutan.' Jason dashed along the lallang edge back to the palms where the stretcher was propped across two crates, and Matsutan turned his head. 'Jason.'

'We're leaving now.'

'I heard. Thank you for coming to see me.'

Jason stood, at a loss for words, so Matsutan spoke for him. 'We succeeded, Jason, and defeated the enemy.'

'Yes.'

Matsutan held out his left hand, and Jason seized it. 'I'll write to you.'

'Yes.' Matsutan answered drowsily and the doctor gave Jason a quick sign. He stepped quietly away and raced back to where the others stood in a group, his apologies ready. But Colonel Chula was listening to a Thai NCO who stood at the salute, reporting, and translated without comment: 'The beach has been searched for half a mile in each direction. No more bodies have been found – nor the bag of money.'

'Yasuno!' Sumitomo grated out the name.

'He may have drowned and been carried out to sea in the storm,' said Jason hopefully, but at a glance from the Japanese detective his optimism died.

'If he comes ashore anywhere along this coast we'll pick him up,' said Colonel Chula grimly, 'dead or alive. Now, Gentlemen!'

They hurried towards the waiting helicopter, past the scattered, dishevelled groups eating breakfast. One group looked familiar, and Jason saw the blue uniform jackets and caps spread out to dry in the sun. From it Captain Chisholm sprang up. 'You're the chap who got out! But what are you doing here? Didn't they send you home?'

'Oh, they let me stay,' replied Jason, pausing in his stride towards the helicopter. He smiled: 'I couldn't just leave you all sitting there!'

'I'm afraid you'll have missed your swimming heats.'

Jason looked at the bruised and bearded face without comprehension. Swimming heats? Then he remembered, and for a moment stared round at the wreckage and the survivors. The swimming heats were part of some life he'd lived in the past, some strange remote existence where television lights had seemed important, and the roar of the crowd the most desirable thing on earth.

'That's not important,' he said, and he meant it. 'I'm sorry you lost your plane,' he added awkwardly.

'Oh, we'll recover it,' said Captain Chisholm confidently. 'We've got Mr Edwards of the airline busy down beside it planning away. He's working out how to bring up pumps, hose away the sand and make a lagoon, and float it out on inflatable rubber bags. Sounds possible, too.'

'Jason!' At a roar and a wave from beside the helicopter he began to walk hurriedly away. 'Got to go, now, all the best –'

Someone seized his hand. 'Jason! We never thought

we'd see you again!' It was Sue, her uniform stained and rumpled, but still somehow workmanlike. 'So you *did* stay! D'you know, I thought you would. But here – two friends to say goodbye.' The two children looked up at him from a spread-out groundsheet. 'Jason,' said the little boy proudly, pleased with himself for remembering, but Margaret studied him without speaking, and he saw realization dawning in her eyes. 'Do you know,' said Sue, 'those hijackers took them off, last night, just before the storm – they were going to take them away!' Her face still showed traces of the fear and despair of the night before.

'I heard something about that. It was terrible.'

'We thought we'd lost them – and then there was all this shooting, out at sea, and we were sure they'd be murdered or drowned. However,' she shook her head as if expunging the memory from her mind, 'they're here and safe, and that's the main thing. Those Thai soldiers did a wonderful job rescuing them.'

'Yes,' said Jason, 'they did.'

'Jason!' The shout was urgent and commanding. 'Get a move on!'

'Can't stop – ' He bent to say good-bye to the children. The little boy took his hand shyly but Margaret gave him a glance, a slightly sideways glance, of total comprehension. She knew; she remembered. He looked her in the eyes and quickly put a finger to his lips. She threw back her head and laughed, and he laughed with her – then turned and ran for the helicopter, Colonel Chula waiting beside it. 'Good-bye for the present, Jason,' he shouted, 'but you will hear from us!'

They shook hands and Jason scrambled up, but as he strapped himself in, he called above the noisy engines: 'There's a white Ipoh tree three hundred yards along the next beach. You'll find something there.'

The Colonel, his black hair blowing wildly in the downward blast, paused and looked hard at him, then shouted back: 'I understand.' He waved and, barely stooping, walked away. Jason waved at his retreating figure and smiled, and he was still smiling to himself when the helicopter took off, swung over the lallang and the palms and rose higher and higher, till below them the beach was once again no more than a fringe to the land, a clean white line between the forest and the sea.

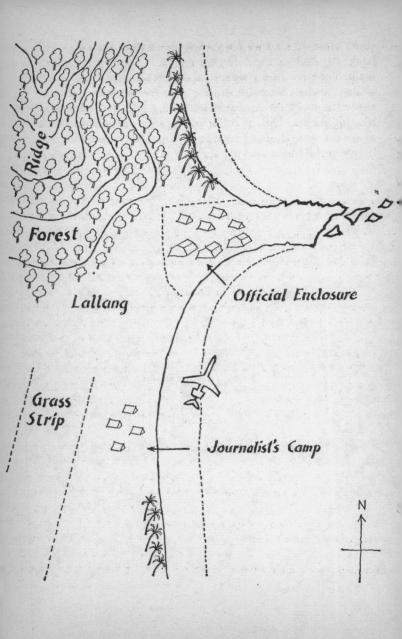

If you have enjoyed reading this book and would like to know about others which we publish, why not join the Puffin Club? You will be sent the club magazine, *Puffin Post*, four times a year and a smart badge and membership book. You will also be able to enter all the competitions. For details of cost and an application form, send a stamped addressed envelope to:

The Puffin Club Dept A
Penguin Books Limited
Bath Road
Harmondsworth
Middlesex